Baker + Taylor 01.19

LITTLE,
BROWN

LB

**LARGE
PRINT**

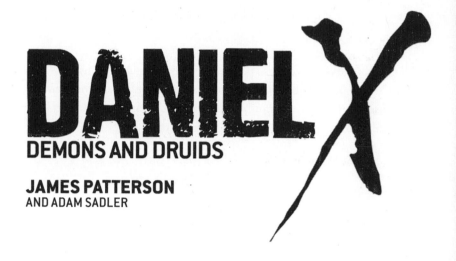

DANIEL X
DEMONS AND DRUIDS

JAMES PATTERSON
AND ADAM SADLER

LITTLE, BROWN AND COMPANY

LARGE PRINT EDITION

Little, Brown and Company

Hachette Book Group
237 Park Avenue, New York, NY 10017
www.lb-kids.com

Little, Brown and Company is a division of Hachette Book Group, Inc. The Little, Brown name and logo are trademarks of Hachette Book Group, Inc.

First Large Print Edition: July 2010

ISBN 978-0-316-08731-5
LCCN 2010922689

10 9 8 7 6 5 4 3 2 1

RRD-C

Printed in the United States of America

For the Jackster—who keeps getting
better by the minute
—JP

DANIEL X

DEMONS AND DRUIDS

PROLOGUE
DON'T TRY THIS AT HOME

I BET I can see London from here, I was thinking.

I was literally 150 feet in the air above a grassy field, outside a charming little village called Whaddon. I'd been in England only a couple of days, and I still had some of that excitement that hits you when you go to a new place—until it turns dangerous and deadly. Which was about to happen in a millisecond.

Because before I had time to take a good look around, I started to fall.

Fast.

Whipping around end over end, I saw the early twilight stars above blurring and the ground rushing up at me like it was about to swallow me whole.

I could hear voices shouting, but it was impossible to tell what they were saying over the blistering wind surrounding me.

Maybe I should have been worried, but I'll admit it—I was enjoying myself. That is, until my good friend Willy kicked me hard in the face.

Willy, Joe, Dana, Emma, and I were playing soccer. Our own version, *in which I was the ball.*

That's correct. I, Daniel X, had transformed myself into a soccer ball. Usually you'll find me in human form, but occasionally I morph. It's just one of my interesting, sometimes flabbergasting powers.

Luckily, soccer balls don't have nerve endings, I thought as I flew back into the air, reaching new heights this time.

"And Willy controls the centered ball beautifully, shooting a deft pass to Joe. He takes it up the line. But—no! Dana sweeps in with a well-executed slide tackle and steals it!" Joe always liked to deliver the play-by-play for our games. And just about anything else we did.

"Pay attention, Joe," said Willy, grimacing. "We're getting creamed by girls."

Dana, in the middle of passing me to the other end of the field, cracked up. Lanky Joe is the least athletic of my four friends, but when he shuts up even he can play soccer better than most of the guys in the World Cup.

Dana kicked me hard, and I once again savored the rush of flying through the night sky — until I saw Emma's pale, round face rushing right toward me. She caught me easily on her forehead, and juggled me there for a moment as she turned to the "goalposts," two towering oak trees at the end of the field.

Then Em bent her small, nimble body back and "headed" me straight up in the air. Way up. I relaxed into free fall. Below me, Dana and super-jock Willy were racing toward the goalposts.

Dana got there first. As I came down, her blond hair twisted around her as she jumped and spun like a top, fell backward, and aimed a scorching scissor kick right at the goal. The teeth-rattling power of her kick took me by surprise.

"GOOOOOAAAAAAL!" screamed Joe

from the other end of the field in his best super-stoked announcer's voice.

I had already overshot the goalposts by at least a hundred feet when I realized I was headed straight into the tree-lined gorge that bordered the field.

I focused for a second, and—without even a "pop" or "zap"—I was back to being myself—a teenage kid—again. I grabbed on to an overhanging tree branch as I flew past.

Hanging one-handed over the gorge, I frowned at Dana. "You did that on purpose, didn't you?" I called to her. "Tried to launch me into the briar patch."

She laughed in the way only she can. "Daniel, you look like a hopelessly depressed orangutan."

Before I could come up with a snappy reply, Joe's voice rang across the field. "Okay, you two, *now* can we get going? London's not going to walk to us! We have a monster to catch."

PART ONE
BLOOD AND SUCKERS

Chapter 1

I JUMPED DOWN from the tree and dusted myself off. You think *playing* soccer is dirty?

Try being the ball.

A couple of minutes later, the five of us were strolling down an English country road that was cuter than a postcard. Our pickup soccer match had been a good distraction, but now it was almost eight and night was starting to fall.

"Well, let's hoof it, guys," I suggested. "In a couple of hours we can find somewhere safe to camp out."

"A couple of hours?" Dana complained.

"Can't you materialize a car for us or something? Teleport us?"

"Too tired," I replied. "Takes a lot of focus. Which I don't have much of after you guys kicked the bejeezus out of me."

A light from behind made us turn around. A large vehicle was approaching and appeared to be slowing down. My friends moved back toward the shadows, ready to disappear if need be.

Fortunately, they didn't have to. As the vehicle pulled up alongside me, I saw that it was a beat-up van, probably large enough to hold ten or eleven. A tiny woman with short gray hair was behind the wheel, wearing a tweed suit that was at least two sizes too big for her.

She rolled down her window and peered with careworn eyes into the darkness behind me. I thought she would ask directions, but instead she asked, "Are you lost, dearies?" I liked the nice smile lines around her mouth. I liked her spacious van even more.

I put on my best harmless-backpacking-tourist face. "I'm afraid we're stranded, ma'am.

We're trying to get to London." *To catch some aliens—Number 3 on The List of Alien Outlaws on Terra Firma, to be exact.*

"Oh, Americans...!" She smiled. "Well, I'm heading that way. Hop aboard."

Chapter 2

IT DIDN'T TAKE MUCH to convince us. We gratefully piled in. Willy and Emma in the back, Dana and me in the middle row, and Joe sprawled out in the passenger seat next to the driver.

We drove in silence for about ten minutes or so. Joe had nodded off, and Willy and Emma, who are brother and sister, were chatting in hushed, lazy voices behind me.

I had almost dozed off when Dana moved her head in close, almost right against my ear.

"Have you noticed anything odd, Daniel?" she whispered.

"What?" I whispered back.

"The driver's seat—it's on the left side."

"So? That's where it's supposed to be."

"Not so. We're in *England,* remember? They drive on the other side."

That was a little unusual, I thought to myself. *Why would the van be American?*

And there was something else, something that had been gnawing at me since we got in. Something about what the driver was wearing. Tweed is a rough grayish green material made of wool. It's most often used for the jackets of college professors, pipe-smoking stamp collectors, and—now I remembered— hunters.

And how did I now guess that the little old lady was not a professor or stamp collector? Call me crazy, but it didn't fit with the profile of those folks to be driving a vehicle that had—I noticed with horror—what appeared to be *dried bloodstains* all over the backseat.

I tried to lean forward to get a better view into the front seat. That's when I realized I couldn't move a muscle. I couldn't even blink.

13

"So you've noticed, *dearie*." The driver's voice seemed to get deeper and rattle in her throat. Then an inhuman rasp twisted its way out. "I'm a hunter. *JUST. LIKE. YOU.* And I do believe I've caught dinner!"

Chapter 3

JOE SNAPPED his head up. Or tried to, I should say. "Dinner? Who said something about dinner?" The guy had an appetite bigger than the British Isles.

"The person who's about to devour you," Emma said through gritted teeth.

"Hey! I can't move, guys," he reported. "Even my mouth feels like it's starting to freeze up."

"Thank God," muttered Dana, but I could hear the fear in her voice.

"Silence!" shouted the driver. It seemed all wrong: that grating, metallic voice coming out of that kindly-looking grandmother's face.

But it wasn't my imagination. In the next instant a gray, pulsating tentacle descended from the ceiling and wrapped itself around my mouth. It felt sticky, warm, and alive. Out of the corner of my eye, I could see a dozen more tentacles gagging my friends. Dana's eyes were flooded with fear and confusion.

Not to be able to explain what was happening—to *her*, most of all—was excruciating. The problem was, I couldn't move, I couldn't create anything, I couldn't transform. I couldn't even talk, to tell my friends to break out, to run away.

If I could have activated my powers, there might have been any number of ways I could have gotten us out of this—by making my friends *disappear*, for instance. (I'll have to explain *that* trick to you later.)

Since I didn't hear another word from my friends, it looked like they were fully incapacitated at this point, too.

I tried to assess our very *sticky* situation. As my eyes scanned the walls of the van I could see them moving, pulsing, *breathing*. And the ceiling — it was a forest of waving tentacles.

Now I understood why we couldn't move our bodies. Strong tendrils that were no thicker than rubber bands had shot out from the van's seats and enveloped our arms and legs more effectively than steel manacles could.

The tentacles reminded me of the sea anemones I used to see in the tide pools on the Oregon coast. Unsuspecting fish who swam too close would be grabbed, stunned by the neurotoxins in the anemones' tentacles, and slowly digested.

That's what this van was, I realized suddenly. *A giant anemone.*

And then came another totally creepy thought: The driver wasn't actually driving. She was part of the alien, one of its organs. She was the bait.

Chapter 4

SHE—*IT,* I should say—saw my look of understanding and horror.

"By now you've noticed my tentacles are full of neurotoxins." *It* cackled nastily. "Just be thankful that you'll all be dead before you're digested. I'm told that the process is excruciating."

The old woman's body began to transform now, melting away into her seat. Meanwhile, a bulbous tentacle tightened around my mouth, and the interior of the van seemed to be *shrinking.*

I blinked, desperately trying to clear my mind and find a quick solution. Being squashed into mush and then digested? Not how I was planning to leave the earth.

Up in the front of the van, Joe's head was shuddering as he struggled against paralysis. Behind me I could hear Willy gurgling and Emma humming in a useless attempt to speak — or scream. And Dana...well, one of her hands had solidified around mine in a death grip of fear.

Hundreds of mouths had opened up *in the walls* around us and began to speak in unison, like a nightmare in surround sound.

"Alien Hunter," the mouths addressed me, "this is for my beloved brother. It's too bad he couldn't be here to see it. Do you remember Number 40? You disintegrated him in Dallas, Texas!"

Of course I remembered! In fact, the oily-smooth interior of the van reminded me all too much of being *inside the stomach* of Number 40 before he — well...that's another story, and I couldn't focus on past victories right now.

The roof was pressing down hard against our heads now. The walls and ceiling constricted like a giant heart beating.

"Nice eating you..." The beast's final message trailed off in a sickening gurgle. "I'm Number 43, by the way. My brother's name was Jasper."

"May he rest in *pieces!*" I wanted to quip.

Another powerful contraction came. The walls closed in even tighter, pushing me and Dana together. It was something I might have enjoyed, if we weren't both about to become meat-and-bone Jell-O pudding.

The despair was overwhelming. It was as if all the terror my friends were feeling was being transmitted back to me times ten. I had never gotten them into a situation this bad before, one that I was powerless to get them out of.

The walls were closing in, bending me double. The tentacle around my throat was twisting too tight for me even to swallow. Everything was getting dim, and quiet, and distant.

It's over, I thought. My eyes were finally squeezed shut and I thought I might suddenly burst like an overripe zit.

And then behind the pain and the fear I heard words way in the back of my mind.

"You still have time...you can take out Number 43. At least I think so."

I recognized the voice immediately. It was my father.

My *dead* father.

Chapter 5

EXCUSE ME while I digress. I was only three when my parents were killed, murdered by one of the most evil alien creatures ever to have set foot on Earth — The Prayer by name — who just happens to be Number 1 on The List. Even in those three short years, though, my parents had managed to fill my brain with all kinds of interesting and useful information, which surfaces from time to time — anything from a fantastic recipe for barbecue sauce (the secret's in the sugar) to, say, the speed you need to travel to escape Earth's gravity (around 25,000 mph). It's usually really simple stuff like that—but sometimes it's the bit of knowledge that could save your skin.

Right now I really, *really* hoped my dead father was about to offer survival tips instead of cooking tips.

"Dad...what? I'm kind of tied up right now," I answered him in my thoughts.

I could still feel the greasy tentacle choking me, feel the wall and ceiling pressing against me, but at least they weren't getting tighter. I wasn't gasping for breath either. Miraculously, I was able to open my eyes.

One at a time.

If I had been able to move the rest of my body I would have reeled in shock. Staring right into my eyes was Dana, her mouth twisted into a circle of horror. But here's the really strange thing: she was *totally* motionless.

I tried to speak, struggled to touch Dana, but my body, my head, my face, were immobilized. Not just paralyzed, but completely frozen.

That's when I realized something that was easily as fascinating as a meeting with the Dalai

Lama. Not only wasn't I suffocating, but I wasn't breathing. Then it hit me.

Time had stopped.

My father's voice rang out again in my skull, stronger this time. "Very good, Daniel. I knew you hadn't forgotten. Even though you were only two when I taught you how to dive below the surface of the flow of time. Well, I'll see you later, champ."

Wait! I thought. *What do I do now?* But my dad's voice was gone.

I had no idea how I'd made time freeze, but my father's words had stirred something—a distant memory. *Rotating stars, spinning planets.*

I remembered Dad hanging a mobile over my crib. A model of Earth's solar system—spinning, slowing, stopping. And then it started to spin in the opposite direction—in reverse. It was all coming back to me, the knowledge slowly trickling in like an Internet download.

Imagine that your brain is a spotlight that casts a sharp focus on whatever you're looking at, or thinking about, or feeling. I had to defocus, widen that beam until it shone on *everything.*

It's even harder than it sounds, and I was out of practice.

Usually when I use my powers, I have to concentrate, but this time it was just the opposite. First I relaxed, let my mind go limp—not an easy feat when the girl you care about most is going to die right before your eyes.

Hold on, Dana.

I felt my brain detach itself from all my sensations right down to the taste of sweat in my mouth. And that's when I saw Dana's left eyelid flicker. Her expression was changing, becoming less terrified, but not in a way I'd ever seen a face change before.

I was turning back time.

Chapter 6

AS DANA'S FEATURES lost their deer-in-the-headlights look, the walls that had been crushing us pulled back into their original shape. The tentacles withdrew from our necks, the poison from our bodies. The sensation in my ears was unexpected, like the twisted sounds of music playing backward. I could actually *feel* the vibrations of the van's motor, as well as my friends' and the little old homicidal lady's voices coming out of my ears.

Then everything started to speed up.

Joe's snores were returning, traveling back into his mouth. I felt Dana's breath near my ear and considered *pausing* things there—you know, just for a second—but as the thought hit me, the moment was gone, and we were all traveling backward out of the van.

Before I knew it we were standing in the road watching it drive away in reverse. Now I had to refocus my mind, to restart time flowing forward again.

I was fully prepared for a mental battle, but as soon as I stopped relaxing my thoughts, I felt a *jolt,* like an elevator stopping too fast in the middle of a thousand-story building. When I turned around I saw Willy, Joe, Dana, and Emma staring at me expectantly from the shadows at the side of the road. They seemed oblivious to the fact that we'd nearly been the alien equivalent of goulash.

I couldn't believe it. I'd actually gone *back in time.* On my first try!

"Is everything all right, Daniel?" asked Dana. "You look a little pale."

"Yeah, you look a little disoriented, you know, like you just saw an *alien,*" Joe quipped. He wiggled his fingers beside his head and started singing the theme from *The Twilight Zone* in a high-pitched falsetto.

"Give him a break, Joe," said Emma. "It's still not too late for us to ditch you here. I hear Whaddon is famous for its delicious pork pies. You'll be in pig heaven."

"Hey, I think somebody's coming," Willy announced, pointing at a set of headlights.

And there it was: the vehicle of death. From here on out, things would be easier without having to worry about my friends—or explaining how I knew exactly what was going to happen next.

Chapter 7

I CUPPED my hands out in front of me and concentrated. I'm no chemistry major, but I've read some textbooks. A few hundred, actually. I quickly visualized the chemical compound I wanted. Two parts nitrogen, oxygen, and hydrogen, and one part carbon. A dash of dioctyl sebacate, a bit of polyisobutylene. *There.*

In my hands, I held a fist-sized lump of explosive.

Even my friends looked a little concerned.

"Uh, Danny Boy? What are you doing there, buddy?" asked Willy.

"I'll tell you guys later. Trust me, it'll be a real blast."

"Huh?" said Willy.

"Daniel—" Dana tried to protest as I made all four of them disappear. (I'll have to explain *that* trick to you later.) It was all I could do not to conjure up a bazooka and simply wait for the van to get within range.

As soon as the explosive was secure, I walked back to where we'd been standing before. The van slowed, and the window rolled down.

"Here I am! Come and get me!" I taunted in my most maniacal voice. *"Dinner's ready!"* I hooted as I tore down the road toward the tree.

The old hag must have floored it because the vehicle lurched forward and roared toward me. And right toward my trap.

Using my lightning-fast reflexes, I was able to slip out of the way right before the van smashed into the tree.

And then I half leapt, half fell backward, just out of range of the expanding fireball.

For a moment, vivid geysers of oranges, reds, and yellows hung in the air—and at the center was the van, burning, vaporizing into atoms. There was a grating, scraping sound under the roar of the shock wave—the alien screaming. And then there was only smoke, and silence, like in a cemetery at three in the morning.

Leaves and ash rained down through the haze. All that was left of the tree was a charred stump a foot or two high. Of the van, *nada*. Well, almost *nada*. A hubcap rolled toward me, dissolving into a puddle of mush before it reached my feet.

Thanks, Dad, I thought to myself. *You saved my life. And we got Number 43.*

Chapter 8

AFTER the carpooling disaster, we got smart and took the train to London. I know it sounds anticlimactic, but when we finally arrived there, the big city looked pretty much how I expected.

Of course, before I left the States I'd speed-read through about twenty travel guides as well as a couple of history textbooks, plus the complete works of Shakespeare for good measure. Frankly, at this point I probably knew more about London than the prime minister or, certainly, the mayor.

But it was thrilling to see in person all the things I'd only read about, like the Tower of

London (not *technically* a tower, but, even better, it's more like a *castle*). Let me debunk a few other common misconceptions for you. *Big Ben*—actually the name of the clock's bell, not the clock itself. *Hyde Park*—London's version of Central Park (or, actually, vice versa)—is *not* named after Dr. Jekyll's alter ego. *Piccadilly Circus*—not nearly as fun as it sounds. Turns out it's just a big intersection. Which was where all five of us were currently cruising around on a double-decker bus.

Emma was kneeling on the seat behind me. "The driver says we'll be at Oxford Circus in a couple of minutes."

"And you've pretty much missed all of the sights since your nose is still buried in that laptop," Dana noted.

"So who's next on our hit list?" Willy asked.

"Not a Lapillajade, I hope," Emma commented, referring to the most intelligent species in the universe. "They're pretty tricky."

"Absolutely not. Most of them are good guys," I said. In fact, Lapillajades are often disguised on Earth as astronomers and scientists, including dudes like Copernicus, Galileo, and Sir Isaac Newton. Humankind would pretty much be in the Dark Ages without them.

I looked back down at the open laptop I had balanced on my knees. If you didn't stare too closely, you might think it was the newest, slimmest iBook. It wasn't much thicker than a sheet of paper, but its technology housed information on every known extraterrestrial outlaw on the planet. Just for the heck of it, I'd even run a search on the van-emone and found out its real name: Ziquechyx Philbin. With a name like that, no wonder the beastie was so angry.

But the reason I'd come to London in the first place was to hunt a sinister alien force who was the polar opposite of a Lapillajade. Primitive, fierce, uncontrollable—and with no intellect whatsoever. And he was *the number three most-wanted alien on Earth.*

Name: Phosphorius Beta
Human Aliases: Bayswater Burnie, The Fleet Street Flamer, Jack the Zippo

Area of Infestation: London and surrounds, United Kingdom, Terra Firma

Arrived on Terra Firma: Unknown. At least half a century ago, but some speculate earlier. Without a witness to verify the presence of the "Dark Heart," as its "soul" is legendarily known, it is often impossible to distinguish Phosphorius Beta from natural fire sources.

Illegal Activities: Arson, Smuggling, Vandalism, Homicide

Planet of Origin: Cyndaris

Alien Species: Phosphorian

Special Abilities: Possession of Human Bodies/Minds, Manipulation of Flame (see Phosphorians)

The file photo that was up on the screen was indistinct, to say the least. In fact, it looked like a distant shot of a field, ablaze with red-tinged flames.

I guess that was to be expected; according to my notes, no human had ever come into close contact with Number 3 and survived—at least in human form.

But that was also to be expected, wasn't it? The List described Phosphorians as follows:

The Phosphorians are the dominant sentient life-form on the volcanic planet of Cyndaris, which orbits the red dwarf star Gliese 876. Not much is known about them, as Cyndaris is utterly inhospitable to organic life. Average surface temperature on the planet is approximately 2000 degrees Kelvin, hot enough to melt titanium.

Phosphorians who venture off-world invariably destroy nearly everything they come into contact with through the process of combustion. Current intelligence indicates that this is due to their physical makeup, which is suspected to consist solely of an exothermic and self-sustaining chemical reaction.

Translation? By The List's account, the Phosphorians were made out of pure flame.

The data went on to describe Beta's rap sheet here on Earth. Most of it, predictably, involved burning things: buildings, crops, vehicles, even people, even pets. The London newspapers had attributed his crimes to three or four different arsonists, but according to the information in front of me, Number 3 was Earth's worst firebug.

I was nervous about facing him, and not just because of my recent encounter with the Death Van. The last time I had a seriously close encounter with fire was when I was three, when the alien named The Prayer killed my parents and burned down our home.

Trust me, that tends to leave an impression that lasts.

Chapter 9

ON ACCOUNT of our house being burned to the ground, the only thing my mom and dad left me—besides The List of Alien Outlaws on Terra Firma—was my new day job: I am the Alien Hunter. Or, as Dana playfully refers to me, "Space Cop Numero Uno."

I guess that deserves an explanation.

Before their murders, my mother and father were Alien Hunters here on Earth, where alien outlaws have lived and created havoc for millions of years. The aliens have been responsible for a few minor mishaps—like one of the ice ages, the extinction of several animal species, and, more recently, the Great Chicago Fire, the fire that destroyed most of the Coney Island amusement park in the early 1900s, countless kidnappings and missing persons — especially kids and, for some reason, dogs. I guess these creeps never read *Marley and Me* or watched any *Lassie* reruns or movies.

There are a couple of other things you need to know about me, too.

First, *my four best friends:* Willy, Joe, Emma, and Dana (who I'm kind of crazy about). Tragically, my friends died years ago on our home planet Alpar Nok as a result of a ruthless planetary annihilator known as Number 6.

Rewind, you're saying. *Didn't they just star in the whole beginning of this story here in the present day?*

Okay, brace yourself for this one: I can re-create them pretty much at will — for companionship, fun, safety, to help pry open sticky jars, and so on and so forth. And Mom and Dad show up sometimes too — along with a little sister (Brenda, affectionately known as Pork Chop) that I never truly had but always wanted.

You see, I happen to have the greatest super-power of them all: *the power to create.*

And no, I'm not God, or a god, or the son of a god.

At least I don't think so.

Chapter 10

"I'M TIRED OF driving to all these circuses that aren't really circuses," complained Joe as we disembarked at Oxford Circus. "Let's find somewhere to crash and have a snack. I could eat a horse! Oh, I mean, *'Scuse me, guvnor, but Oi declare Oi could eat a 'orse!'*"

"Don't be disgusting, Joe," said Emma, giving him a look. Emma was fanatical about animals of all kinds, unless they were deadly alien life-forms.

"Yeah," I added. "And your cockney accent could use some work. Try watching *Mary Poppins* again."

At Oxford Circus we were near the center of town, and the heart of the action: just a few blocks from the West End, where the theaters are, and Soho, which is full of restaurants and nightclubs. I figured even an alien and his imaginary friends wouldn't seem too weird in the middle of a bunch of ravers, actors, and dancing fools. This, I had decided, was where we should set up our home base.

We split up in order to find our perfect abode. I told my buds to look for something empty but not derelict. Over the past couple of years we'd done this many times, so they knew what to look for.

The best part about doing things this way was that, even though we were scattered all over the area, we could talk to one another telepathically. It's like a chat room in your head, and everybody's invited.

Twenty minutes passed, and then I heard Willy's voice coming over my mental intercom. "How would you feel about staying in a youth hostel, Daniel? I hear they're supercheap."

"Stay with a bunch of grungy backpackers?

No, thanks," Emma jumped in. "Those folks don't ever shower. Sorry. I'm a prude about cleanliness. You know me."

"Hey, I found a little office building that's condemned," said Joe. "Looks cozy."

Dana chimed in. "Yeah, Joseph, if you like floors that have more holes than Swiss cheese. Listen, guys, meet me at the corner of D'Arblay and Berwick. I think I found something really interesting."

It took me a couple of minutes to get to the building Dana had found. It was a two-story town house covered top to bottom with tarps and scaffolding. One look at the place and I could tell that construction had been halted for quite some time.

"And this is better than my condemned office building because...?" Joe scoffed.

"Because, let's face it, girls have a better sense of interior design," Dana shot back. "I'm not game to sleep in icky gray office cubicles if I don't have to. You'll see what I mean."

REFURBISHED 2-BEDROOM! CONTACT OWNER FOR DETAILS! screamed a faded sign in the window. Underneath it were the words READY FOR MOVE-IN ON . . . and a series of dates that had been crossed out. The last one was over three months ago.

I shut my eyes for a moment, concentrating, visualizing. Iron and carbon, beaten thin. When I opened them, I was holding two of my favorite tools, a lock pick and a tension wrench.

"Guys," I said, as I leaned under a tarp and popped the lock, "welcome to our humble abode."

Chapter 11

AS A SIDE DOOR swung open silently, I was hit with a blast of stale air. I've been in a lot of abandoned buildings, and with the help of my eight alien senses I can tell a lot by taking one whiff of a place.

"Hmm...atmosphere's dry. I guess we're mold-free," I said. "Overtones of wood polish. Slight bouquet of musty cotton stuffing. Can anyone tell me what that means?"

"Yeah, baby! We've got *furniture!*" cried Joe delightedly, running across the room and throwing himself sideways onto a richly upholstered couch that had gold claws for feet. "So, do I look like Rose from *Titanic*? 'Oh, paint me, Jack, paint me —'"

Joe broke off into a laughing and coughing fit so violent that he rolled off the couch and onto the floor.

"I still don't see why we can't just rent a normal place, Daniel," said Willy, wiping tears of laughter from his eyes. "That's what we did in LA, remember?"

I hesitated. I had told them about the venome and my discovery of time travel, but I hadn't mentioned just how close we'd all been to becoming alien hash.

"I just want to make sure we're off Number 3's radar. Totally off the radar," I replied with a little too much emphasis on the dangerous aspects of this gig.

"But—"

"Look," I continued, "call me paranoid if you want, but I'm talking complete stealth, okay? You guys gotta promise me," I added. "Seriously."

There was an awkward silence, finally broken by Dana. "Daniel, do you want to talk about it? Maybe you should..."

I didn't really, but I gave a nod anyway. I ignored the slight feeling of guilt creeping up on me as I made Emma, Joe, and Willy vanish from the scene. Where exactly do they go? I don't know; they won't tell me.

Then I followed Dana upstairs into one of the bedrooms.

Wow, I thought, *we hit the jackpot, didn't we?* In the center of the room was a gigantic four-poster bed, complete with lush red curtains. A wardrobe roomy enough to hold the clothes of a total shopaholic stood off to one side; next to it hung a luxuriously tall and wide mirror. On the other walls, a series of large sun-bleached tapestries depicted knights endlessly hunting a white stag.

The two of us sat down on the bed. Dana looked at me expectantly.

"Well?" she said.

"Well, what?" I said stupidly.

"Tell me what's going on."

"Um...how about alien hunting?" I offered. "Same old, same old?"

"It's different this time," Dana insisted. "I

47

remember what happened in the van, Daniel. The walls were crushing us; I couldn't breathe. I was in pain, the worst I've ever felt. All I could do was stare at you, knowing we were going to die. *We were all going to die.* And then you saved us."

She lowered her voice a little, as if the rest of our friends were in the next room, listening. "I don't think the others know about the time travel. Or why you're a little shaky right now."

"Well, frankly I'd rather they didn't."

Her voice was gentle. "Daniel, it's all right. It's all part of what you have to do. What you were born to do, I suppose. We're just along for the ride. Right?"

"Dana, there's something else...something else that's been getting to me." I was definitely in spilling-your-guts mode. I knew I would have to watch myself, or I might just get all gooey on her about how crazy I really was about her.

"You..." I swallowed nervously, unable to speak for a moment. Then I regained my voice. "You *were* real. Back on my—our—homeworld, Alpar Nok. You, Joe, Willy, Emma. You were all real."

Her expression went from surprised to baffled to horrified.

I went on. "When I visited there I saw images, like telepathic snapshots. My relatives showed me. We were all kids who hung out together, before I left for Earth. Then the Vermgypians came, invaded. They called it FirstStrike. You were all...killed at your school..."

The silence seemed to fill up the room, till I thought we would both drown in it. Then Dana's voice, shaking a little, pulled me back to the surface. She spoke slowly, like she was trying to solve a tough math problem.

"So we were real, then we died. I don't remember any of it. What does that make us? *Ghosts?*"

"I don't know, Dana. All I do know is, I'll never, ever let any of you die again." I had to fight to keep my eyes from tearing up. "I swear, on the Bible, on The List, on the house where I grew up—except I can't because it's burned down. But never, never again will my friends be hurt." Then I looked up into her perfect blue eyes. "Especially not you, Dana."

She stared right back at me with the softest smile in the history of this planet.

"Thank you, Daniel. I'll try to do the same for you. I would die for you. *Again*."

Chapter 12

I LAY BY MYSELF on the bed for a while, staring like a zombie at the wood-beamed ceiling. A million thoughts raced through my head, way too fast for me to comprehend. I'd dropped a little bit of a bomb on Dana, and she'd needed some alone time, so I made her disappear.

But after that convo, I still needed someone to talk to, worse than ever.

Then I felt a reassuringly familiar hand on my shoulder. "Daniel?"

"Mom?"

I hadn't intentionally created her, but there she was. She was wearing a purple knit cardigan with yellow puppies on it, one of her favorites. Sometimes, when I needed her most, she would just appear. I'd created her and my father so many times that it had become reflexive.

"Feeling down? You shouldn't be. You know that you have friends and family who love you very much. Even if they are imaginary."

I couldn't help smiling. For people who had been killed almost thirteen years ago, my parents had a lighthearted view of the world.

"Thanks, Mom. Hey, did you know I can time-travel?"

"You were the last one to figure that one out, sweetie. It's okay. I always told your father you were a late bloomer." She gave a little giggle, and then suddenly got serious. "But that's not the reason I'm here, is it?"

She was my mother, all right. Her mind-reading abilities weren't really fair play, though—she was my creation, after all. I could never really know for sure, but I suspected she might have access to parts of my brain, my memory, my subconscious, that even I didn't know about.

"It's just...when Dana, and the others, almost died back there, things changed somehow. I'd never felt like that about my friends before. Losing them would be...almost as bad as losing you and Dad all over again."

"You could just conjure them up again, Daniel. They're already dead."

"No. You don't get it, Mom. It's about doing the wrong thing. It's about hurting them. It's just...I don't ever want to put them in danger again."

"You know I love your friends, Daniel. But you can't let yourself be distracted. Number 3, Beta, he's the real deal. You've never faced a power quite like his."

"Yeah, I've been studying him."

"Well, your father did too," she said. "He's been an infestation in this country and on this planet for far too long."

I was intrigued. "But The List dates his history back only about fifty years. He came to Terra Firma before that?"

"You'll have to figure that one out yourself. Just remember, if you want to play with fire you have to accept the consequences. *You will get burned.* Trust me on that."

I nodded. I could take getting burned if it meant keeping my friends safe.

She gave a wry smile. "Daniel, you're quite the Alien Hunter already, but I don't know if you're ready for Beta. Your father and I met him once. Think of a million or so angry, hungry wolves—on fire. That's a pretty good approximation of Number 3."

And on that scary note—she was gone again.

Chapter 13

I BARELY SLEPT all night. I couldn't shake my mom's words. Instead, I went into an almost obsessive trance, reading links off Google News—anything that had to do with fire. I wondered just how often Beta was at the center of any and all destructive fires around the world. And there were a lot of them.... Wildfires, worse than ever in recorded history. Factory fires, mine fires, apartment building fires, churches and clinics and homes set on fire by missing arsonists...

Feeling totally overwhelmed, I reread The List description again. It placed Beta in the British

Isles only. So why would he *stay* here? Most aliens I knew couldn't wait to get their slimy little hands all over the globe.

I asked my friends the same question over a breakfast of cold pizza the next morning. No offense to the Brits, but their pizza sometimes leaves a bit to be desired. Willy had already tossed his slice in the garbage and instead was jury-rigging a TV set to work on the kitchen counter.

"Maybe Beta has a personal thing against England," Dana said as a joke.

"Maybe he had a French relative," Willy suggested. Not the most culturally sensitive comment.

"Or got bad gas from some blood pudding," Joe offered.

"I'm serious, guys. Why not go burn down the whole Amazon rain forest, for Pete's sake? Kill the world's oxygen supply? Or go to one of the poles and start melting the ice caps faster than they're already going? He could do some real damage."

"Speaking of real damage...," Emma began, and her brother finished:

"Maybe he *is*. Check this out." The picture had just flicked on to *BBC News*. And it was big, bad news.

Within the past hour or so there had been a giant explosion at a factory outside London. The flaming debris had scattered across a wide area and set fire to dozens of workers' homes that were clustered nearby...and a school and day-care center.

That part drew gasps from all of us.

So far all that was known was that there were likely hundreds of victims, and it was too early to determine just how many of those were children. But the news was expected to be grim. And of course there was no indication of a cause yet.

A highly dramatic shot of billowing flames and smoke that reminded me of the aftermath of a volcanic eruption was replayed over and over, and helicopters in the area showed the guts of the factory spewed across a vast radius. It was truly a horrific sight.

On a hunch, I dashed over to The List computer and tried to find the image of massive smoke and flame on the BBC website.

As you might imagine, my high-tech alien brainbox had extraordinary resolution and magnification capabilities, and I clicked fast to zoom in as much as possible to ground zero of the explosion.

"Oh my goodness," Emma whispered when she saw a peculiar black shape take form.

"More like, oh my *evilness*," Joe corrected, shaking his head in disbelief as we all saw the suggestion of eyes, and *teeth*.

"Not funny," I said. "At all."

"What is it?" Dana asked, leaning over me to peer at the screen and putting her hands on my shoulder. I took a wild guess.

"The Dark Heart."

Chapter 14

WE DISCUSSED heading to the site of the explosion for clues on Beta but, after some discussion, decided that it wasn't the right thing to do. The entire area would be teeming with police investigators, medical professionals, and grieving families. And if we'd seen what we thought we'd seen, we knew the "perpetrator" would already have left the scene of the crime.

So where would a Phosphorian hang out?

That's how I decided we would split up to investigate different "hot spots"—literally—in the city. Factories that needed flame in their processing, for instance. And if Beta had servants—locals to help with the parts of his fuel-harvesting operation not involving, you know, burning things up—they'd probably be the kind of folks who were used to working with fire.

Emma and I went to a metal workshop in the south part of London. I'd brought Emma with me instead of Dana this time since I sensed she was feeling a little left out of my inner circle of one. She'd figured out that the night before I hadn't "disappeared" Dana at the same time as I'd gotten rid of the rest of them.

My face broke into a smile when we arrived. The sign outside this workshop read B. FAUST AND COMPANY, LTD., the inscription under a picture of a jolly-looking blacksmith with his arms crossed. I had a good feeling about this: Having read most of the great European classics at least once by now, I gathered that there was a real *devil* running this place. (Look up "Faust" on Wikipedia if you want to know more.)

Emma and I peeked in through a paned window in the front door. The place was incredible: a cavernous, dark room lit only by giant furnaces along two walls. The air inside was alive with sparks and the crackle of arc welders.

A nearby figure lifted its welding mask. I was surprised to see a lean, grizzled middle-aged woman's face looking out at us. Grimacing, actually.

"Oi, no kids in here!" she shouted in a gravelly voice, opening the door and giving us a fiery glare. "Go 'way."

I put on my innocent wouldn't-hurt-a-fly face. "Sorry, ma'am, we're just doing a school report on—"

"Something wrong with your hearing, sonny? I said get out! Now, if you know what's good for ya—go!"

We blinked our way back out into the sunlight a few paces from the workshop.

"Well, that seemed promising," remarked Emma. "She had a sort of, um, *alienesque* rudeness about her."

I shrugged. "Dunno. Maybe she's just a garden-variety humanoid jerk."

I hated to admit it, but I wasn't sure exactly what we were looking for. Ashes? Burn marks?

Overdone steaks? This may not be what you want to hear from the Alien-Hunter-slash-Guardian-of-Earth, but sometimes it's the bad guys who find *me*.

Like that stupid van, I chided myself for the thousandth time, still feeling dumb about the careless move. I couldn't get it out of my head.

"Everything all right?" asked Emma solicitously, putting her hand on my shoulder.

I pulled away, then immediately felt bad as I saw her mouth and eyes droop at the corners. "Yeah, I'm just fine, Em. Come on, let's see if there's a back door," I said, trying to inject some softness into my voice.

But then Emma suddenly grabbed my arm, her hand as tight as a pincer.

"What—?" I started to say, but she cut me off.

"Don't turn around, Daniel," she said softly but urgently. "We're being watched. And the creep watching us is definitely no 'garden-variety jerk.'"

Chapter 15

WHATEVER MINOR COMPLAINTS I might have about Emma—likes animals more than people, overly optimistic to the point of drowning us all in sunbeams—there was one thing for sure: that girl has a bloodhound's nose when it comes to sniffing out bad guys.

Unfortunately, even though I'm an alien, I don't have eyes in the back of my head. One time in Texas I had to fight an Argusian, a slimy fish-reptile with giant eyes not just on the back of its head, but also on its knees and elbows and on each of its enormous *teeth*. That was not an easy beast to sneak up on.

Now I turned a little to face the wall behind us, casually leaning against it with one hand. Then I focused all my energies into the wall's surface. This was a relatively easy one: *clay to silicate.* As soon as I had the thought, one of the bricks, up at my eye level, shimmered and became a rectangular mirror.

I scanned the mirror's reflection of the street behind me. "Aviator sunglasses? Cancer stick?" I said.

"That's the creep itself," Emma whispered back.

The guy was sitting on a bench across the street from the foundry, smoking a cigarette. He was throwing us the most casual glances, but when I paid attention, well, even behind the shades, those glances were as piercing as a switchblade.

"Now *that* looks like a man who works with fire," Emma said, referring to the man's barrel-like arms, scarred and pitted with burns.

I nodded. "But maybe he's just an employee taking a smoke break," I suggested, even though I'd already convinced myself that he was one of Beta's followers. It's an alien-radar thing I've got going on. Somehow, the cretin had already found me.

I heard a familiar roar in my ears, the sound made by the engine of one of those double-decker buses. A lucky break for a getaway. I cocked my head toward Emma. "Hop on my back."

As the bus passed between us and the man with the Popeye arms, Em jumped up onto my back and I sprinted out behind the bus, using it for cover. I kept up a comfy thirty miles per hour or so until the double-decker rounded the corner. Then I skidded to a stop.

I peeked back toward the metal workshop. The guy was looking around, perplexed by our sudden disappearance. Maybe he was only human after all.

He shook his head, stood up, tossed his filthy cigarette butt away, grinding it out with a thick boot heel, and pulled a fresh one out of the pack in his breast pocket. I hate littering almost as much as smoking, but in the next moment I forgot about the crudhead's misdemeanor.

Casually glancing around him, he cupped an

empty hand. Then he bent his head down and lit his cigarette off a small red flame the size of a strawberry.

The fire was coming right out of his palm.

Did I say he was human? Whoops.

Chapter 16

"FOLLOW THAT CAD," said Em with a wink, and I did. But we stayed well back from Mr. Handfire as he strode away from his post on the bench. He was grumbling to himself, looking around, it seemed, for a stray dog or cat to kick.

"He let us get away. Now he's in tro-u-ble," I whispered in a singsong voice.

After a few blocks, he turned down a cobblestoned alley, tossing his still-lit cigarette into a trash barrel. What a genius. I blinked a few handfuls of water into existence and stopped for a moment to dump it on the trash fire he'd started.

Emma and I got to the alley mouth just in time to see him going through a dingy green door at the far end. After a couple of minutes a shadow flickered in the window of a third-floor apartment. The rusted fire escape that climbed the side of the building was only nine feet or so off the ground, so I jumped up to grab the bottom rung. Michael Jordan's got nothin' on me.

I looked down at Emma as I started to climb. "I'll be right back."

She rolled her eyes. "You afraid it's too dangerous for me?"

"No. If I lose my grip you're going to break my fall." Fortunately, she chuckled. She knew I wouldn't let her get hurt. I could whip up a trampoline or something to fall onto if I needed to.

The ladder was rickety, and the balconies above it looked like they were cobbled together from coat hangers and pipe cleaners. This place was in dire need of a visit from *Extreme Makeover: Home Edition.*

Somehow, I made it to the third floor without getting speared by one of the rusted, broken balcony rails and contracting tetanus. I edged along the wall and looked into the lit window.

The glass was encrusted with grime and cracked in several places, so I had to put my face right up to the window to see through it. *Yowza! Now we're making progress.*

Inside was a kitchen, the messiest I'd ever seen on Earth. Everything was covered with at least an inch of dirt, mildew, garbage, and rotting food. He stood at the stove, wearing a stained apron that read I ♥ GRILLING as he stirred something thick, dark, and lumpy in a saucepan.

I thought I knew every travesty the Brits had unleashed on the culinary world — haggis, spotted dick, good old-fashioned mincemeat — but this didn't even look like food. Unless it was food that had been already eaten, if you know what I mean.

He grabbed a bottle from the counter and poured half of the contents into the pan. Then he lifted the bottle to his mouth and took a swig. Did that label say CASTOR OIL? No, wait. I blinked.

That wasn't right.

I squinted through the glass and put my hands up by the sides of my face to get a better look.

Yup. The bottle's label said CASTROL. He was drinking motor oil.

And that's when — in the middle of another swig — he turned and saw me crouching on the fire escape.

No problem: I ♥ FIGHTING ALIENS.

Chapter 17

THE CREEP must have recognized me, because he choked on his motor oil in mid-swig and started spluttering. Once he regained his composure he squinted his eyes and gave me a steely glare.

"So yah spoh'ed me earlier, eh? Won't say Oi'm surproised." His voice came clearly through the cracks in the window, a perfect cockney accent. Joe definitely needed to take diction lessons from this guy. "'E said yah were one to watch out for."

"'E? You mean *he?*"

"The livin' foire. Yah know, *Betah*!"

"Beta . . . he knows I'm here?" It wasn't actually a question. The way things had been going lately, I wasn't surprised in the least.

"'E knows lotsa things. Like he knows Oi'm gonna kill yah. 'E told me so 'imself."

"Why would you work for an evil maniac like him?" I asked, stalling. You'd be amazed how well this tactic works with dumb criminals. They really love to talk about themselves.

"Well, lemme put it this way for yah, mate. 'E gives me certain . . . *benefits.*"

He put a hand up to his face, and I noticed he was gritting his teeth, hard. Then he raised his sunglasses. His left eye was yellowed and watery. Where his right eye should have been, there was only an empty socket.

I barely had time to register this, when the right side of his face began to swell, and his mouth opened in a primal scream. "Loike this one, f'rinstance!"

Before I could react, a glowing, flaming ball of lava burst from his eye socket, shattered the window, and exploded like a lightning bolt against my chest.

And in case you're wondering, yeah, that hurts even an alien.

I flew backward into the flimsy safety railing. Actually, safety railing was a misnomer — peanut brittle would have done a better job at keeping me safe. The rail buckled instantly, and I went over the side in a cloud of broken glass and rusty metal, flailing my arms in a poor imitation of the backstroke as I fell.

I might have morphed myself into a bird if I hadn't been in excruciating pain from the burn of the flaming eyeball strike. Not to mention that a three-story fall goes extremely fast. There was no way to focus.

I clutched my chest and braced myself for a hard, painful, possibly fatal landing on the cobblestones below. The cobblestones of London's streets had been handpicked to withstand cart wheels, horses' hooves, wheelbarrows. They'd lasted hundreds of years. In a contest with my spine, they were probably going to win.

I gulped, maybe the last thing I would ever do.

Of course, I'd forgotten all about Emma. She hadn't forgotten about me, though. *"DANIEL!"*

Smackdown.

Not many people would let themselves be clobbered to save a friend. Em was brave, I'll give her that. I ended up on top of her, facedown. She wheezed like she'd been punched in the gut fifty times.

"You okay?" I asked her, feeling awful. I didn't *mean* to use her as a cushion. I'd only been joking earlier.

"I might be better if you'd eaten less fish and chips in the past few days," she razzed me. "A few pounds less g-force would have been nice."

I disentangled myself and stood up, pulling Em to her feet as I did.

"I'm guessing your meeting didn't go so well," she said.

"Well, actually, it was a blast."

I could feel blood running down my face where a shard of glass had cut my forehead. A circular singe mark was smack-dab in the middle of my chest. My whole body felt like a giant blister.

"We've got to get out of here," I whispered urgently. "You good to run?"

"Run, no. Stumble, okay. Good thing you're

not any heavier or I would have been a rut in the pavement."

As the two of us lurched away as best we could, I heard a demented voice echoing down the alley behind us.

"Don' go, Alien Hunter! Oi just put dinner on! Didn' Oi tell yah, OI HEART GRILLIN'?"

Chapter 18

WHEN WE GOT BACK to the town house that evening, Dana, Joe, and Willy immediately dropped their jaws.

"Wow! What happened?" asked Joe. "Wait, let me guess. Accidentally shot out of a cannon?"

"Almost," Emma said wryly. Dana rushed out of the room to get either first-aid supplies or holy oils for the last rites.

"You both look like mega-crap," contributed Willy. "Are you all right, Em?" He enveloped her in a tight hug. The two of them are so different that sometimes I forget they're brother and sister.

I tried to fake a war-hero pose. "Nothing a few months of R and R wouldn't cure," I said, not wanting to let on how I'd dumped — literally — on Emma. Willy'd never let me live that down. "Em was great. She's due for some vacation time."

"He got blasted off a third-story balcony," said Emma matter-of-factly. "I caught him." Way to blow my plan, Emma.

Joe slapped his hands to the sides of his face. "Great balls of fire!"

"More like eyeballs of fire," I said with a grimace.

Dana came back with a damp towel, sat down beside me, and started to clean the dried blood from my face.

"Did you find Beta?" she asked, wincing in sympathy. "Kind of looks like maybe you did."

"No, not exactly Beta." I fingered the burns in my shirt and furrowed my eyebrows. "You guys have any luck?"

Willy rolled his eyes. "We followed a guy halfway across London because Joe thought he looked 'suspicious.' Turned out he ran a fish-and-chips shop."

"You forgot to mention that his fish-and-chips were spectacular," said Joe.

Dana stared daggers at him. "I swear, Joe, next time one of your 'hunches' leads us to a restaurant, I'm going to put *you* on the menu."

Even though I was exhausted, I joined in their laughter. The happy chorus of their voices reminded me why I put up with the beatings, the kidnappings, all the pain and suffering that came with the territory of hunting outlaw aliens.

My friends reminded me of what I had to lose, what we all had to lose.

Chapter 19

JOE FINALLY FOUND a first-aid kit in the downstairs bathroom, which gave me an excuse for another twenty minutes or so of medical treatment.

Eventually, though, the exhaustion was overwhelming, and I had to say good night to my friends. As I started to climb the stairs, I paused and turned. They were all staring at me. "Uh... guys? Did you—"

We had all heard it. A fluttering sound at the back of the town house, like a giant moth beating itself against a porch light. A humongous alien moth. Maybe a fire-breathing one?

"Daniel, you weren't followed, were you?" Dana's expression was serious, and a little scared. I was still aching all over, but I remembered my promise: I would never let anything hurt her, or the others. *Anything.*

Including a flying dragon, if that's what it was.

I shook my head and motioned for them to keep quiet. Then I crept over to the window at the rear of the room. There was absolutely no movement outside.

The window creaked just a little as I slid it open. I cautiously stuck my head out into the night air.

Still nothing. *So where's Big Bird at?*

There was a nervous knot in my stomach that wouldn't go away, but I was hurting and tired. I couldn't chase every sound I heard, even though there *were* monsters outside the window sometimes, in my closet, occasionally under my bed, inside the toilet once, even in a toothpaste tube, believe it or not.

I finally left my friends on watch and continued upstairs, this time for real. I fell asleep almost at once.

It couldn't have been much later that a loud sound jarred me awake. I was instantly alert and on my feet. In my life, a few seconds of disorientation can make the difference between being alive and seeing an alien's lower intestine in extreme close-up.

Then I heard the noise again: a knocking coming from *inside* the massive wardrobe.

I didn't think I'd been followed. We'd been careful. Beta might know I was in town, but he didn't know where I was living...or we'd be dead already.

Steeling myself, I crept over to the wardrobe and took one carved knob in each hand. In one fluid motion, I threw open the doors.

The wardrobe was empty.

But before I could even breathe a sigh of relief, I felt inhumanly strong hands grabbing me, pinning my arms. *Not good.*

At the same time a wiry arm encircled my neck in a sleeper hold. *Very, very not good.*

I felt hot breath in the hair on the back of my neck. Then an oily, aristocratic voice spoke softly beside my ear, in almost a whisper.

"Well, well, well. Look, lads. I've caught me an Alien Hunter."

Chapter 20

I TURNED to face my captor. The voice matched its owner's face: as smooth as silk, as taut as a piano wire. Kind of handsome, actually. Like a young George Clooney—with spiky hair, dyed blond, if you can imagine *that*. Not, as Emma would say, very "alienesque."

"Well, at last! Snow White's awakened from her slumber!"

I didn't recognize this one from The List. But if he knew about aliens, he was at least in cahoots with one or more. Not with Beta, though— there's no way he could've stayed so *clean*. A tailored white suit was buttoned onto his slender frame, and I recognized the shoes as designer Ferragamos. And he was short, like thirteen-and-just-hit-his-growth-spurt short. He looked like he'd never needed a shave in his life.

But his dark eyes, *in which no pupils were visible,* had the depth of an oil well. Looking into them was like staring into a black hole.

Maybe one that descended all the way to *the everlasting fires.*

Chapter 21

"WHO ARE THEY, DANIEL?" Dana asked. I looked around, startled. She and the rest of my friends, who must have come upstairs to investigate, were being held in a semicircle by four thuggish, tattooed men. The panic in Dana's voice brought back unpleasant memories of nearly seeing the life crushed out of her by alien tentacles.

Another male meathead was holding my arms behind me in a grip of iron. Make that titanium. This guy was practically wrenching my sturdy Alparian arms out of their sockets. It hurt, and I could barely concentrate on what their sleazebag leader was saying, let alone try to make a move on him.

"*Who are we?* Well, that's an interesting question, darling."

Darling? Dana and I both glared at him. The anger helped me focus through the pain. "You better stop right there, before you say anything you're going to regret later."

"Now, now, Daniel." The words slithered off his tongue. "First, let us get straight who's entitled to be angry here. We've been roosting in this lovely abode for the past month or so, and I daresay it was rather rude of you to invite yourselves to our little party."

"I don't *do* manners with hooligans," I spat.

"Hooligans! Heavens, Daniel. I'm just trying to have a civil conversation, so let's not get overheated and do anything rash, like, say, trying to use your creative powers."

I blinked. How did he —

"Oh yes, I know all about you. If you so much as think about making anything, other than making *nice,* of course, your friends here will suffer a very nasty, very permanent accident. I move quickly, and I cut deep."

I seethed silently. He didn't seem to know that I'd been trying desperately to use my powers ever since the moment I'd gained consciousness. The simple fact was that *I couldn't.* My injuries from the fall plus the ache in my arms were making it impossible. I kept trying to concentrate, to summon a baseball bat, a rope, a rock—any-thing—but the physical pain kept sweeping in and disrupting things.

"Now, as to the delicious young lady's ques-tion," our captor continued. "Who are we? I bet Daniel here knows us. And if he doesn't, he should. After all, we know an awful lot about *him.*"

He let out a long, loud laugh—more like a cackle—and I saw into his mouth for the first time.

I'm no dentist, but, well…I know when something is off, and this guy had a prob-lem that would have driven any orthodontist into early retirement. I could see his canines.

They extended a good two inches below the gum line.

And suddenly I knew the answer to Dana's question.

"Great. We've been caught by vampires," I said. I heard Emma gasp.

"Please," said the man in the white suit in an immensely pleased tone. "We prefer to be known as the 'dentally challenged.' You can call me Vlad. And no — I'm not trying to be funny."

Chapter 22

"VLAD? As in, *Dracula?*" I said incredulously. "And I guess Frankenstein's monster and the Wolf Man are waiting outside?"

"Oh, Daniel, you should know that all those stories are just...just...romanticized versions of the truth. Now," he continued, rubbing his hands in anticipation. "Your dossier was right when it said you had quite a brain. And we'll be seeing that brain up close and personal soon enough. Or tasting it."

Ah, now I remembered. This was something I *had* seen mentioned in The List. "You're part of the species *Vampirus sapiens*. And as I recall, it's not blood you're after. You subsist off the cerebral fluids of other creatures. You're brain suckers. I guess Phosphorius Beta sent you to finish us off."

"Beta? That nutter? Never!" For the first time, irritation crossed his features. "I should think he sent *you* here to finish *me* off. After all, we go back centuries, Mr. Beta and I . . ."

"Wait a minute. Beta's been around for *centuries?*" I asked. As long as I was in this freak's capture, I was going to get some information from him.

"Longer than me, in fact. Unfortunately for the old bloke, I'm one of the few who are impervious to his barbaric hunting method. Drives him quite mad indeed, and he knows how to hold *quite* a grudge, that one. He would need to hire a mercenary such as you, Mr. X, to see me gone. You have quite unique methods at your disposal, and I shouldn't like to take the risk of having you employ them."

"I gather from your expensive tastes that it's more likely you're after the bounty on my head." I faked a yawn.

"Not the bounty, my friend—just your head. Your delectable brain, to be exact."

Chapter 23

I WOULD HAVE LAUGHED at this guy if I hadn't seen this part as plain as day: his fangs were growing longer, right before my very eyes.

"Wow," Joe remarked with a low whistle, typically unfazed by it all. "Those babies must be good for skull busting."

"Human brain is quite common and fatty," Vlad explained to us. "Alparian cerebellum, however, is quite the delicacy. I've been seeking it for quite some time."

He slowly started taking his jacket off, as if it were part of his fine-dining ritual. Then he began unbuttoning his shirt cuffs and folding them up. I was expecting a giant lobster bib to come out next.

I could take this nutbag, I knew I could. But I couldn't risk my friends again. I had to make them disappear. Why wasn't it working?

"Well, this has been great, great fun," Vlad went on. "But I've worked up quite an appetite. I'm famished and so is my motley crew."

As I watched, two more fangs sprouted from his gums, then two more. And suddenly his suit darkened to gray, his whole body drew together like a crumpled Kleenex, and his feet came right off the floor.

You've got to be kidding me.

Faster than fire spreading across the surface of a puddle of oil, Vlad morphed from a diminutive creep in a white suit into a giant bat, hovering on wings at least six feet across. His mouth was now bristling with three-inch fangs, fifteen to twenty of them, enough to take a good chunk out of my skull. *Diaemus youngi,* I thought. A white-winged vampire bat. Only this one was about twice as big as it should be.

"Neat," I said bleakly. "I'm impressed."

Generally speaking, bats *squeak*. After all, they're basically flying rats. But the voice that emerged through Vlad's three-inch fangs was deeper and raspier than before. Think Darth Vader with a head cold.

"Enough chitchat. It's time for dinner now. Renfield, if you'd do the honors."

The brain-sucking hulk behind me forced me down to my knees as my friends looked on, horrified. They'd never seen me so powerless. Suddenly the top of my head felt way too exposed.

"Are you sure you wouldn't prefer a low-cal smoothie, Vlad?" I said.

His resonant voice became a little less self-satisfied. "That was so humorous, I thought I'd never start laughing."

I recalled the words from The List's information on vampires: crosses, garlic, holy water, wooden stakes, sunlight.

Wood, I thought. *Wood is easy. Wood, I can do.*

I blocked the pain out of my mind and unleashed all my energies toward the center of the room. In a flash, a giant wooden cross appeared, planted firmly in the floor like some kind of weird tree.

Vlad-Bat reeled backward...and then began laughing hysterically.

Oh, right. Now I remembered the rest of it. Crosses, garlic, holy water, wooden stakes, sunlight. *None of these "fictional solutions" are considered effective against* Vampirus sapiens. *The only consistently reliable tactic when dealing with this cruel and deadly species of vampire is to avoid them at all costs.*

Great. Thanks a lot, List.

But then I realized that the thug twisting my arms behind me was laughing too. Laughing so hard that his grip had loosened just a bit.

Just enough?

Chapter 24

YES. I'd played stupid long enough for Hulky to let down his guard. I threw one of my elbows backward as powerfully as I could. There was a startled "oof!" from behind. Before he could take firm hold again, I was already busy carving changes in reality.

I jumped high in the air and, almost instantly, felt myself transform. Yahoo! Before the giant bat or his henchmen could make a move, I had spread eight-foot wings of my own. I was hovering, too.

I had changed myself into a hawk—one about as large as a lion.

The vampires recoiled at the powerful gusts from my wings. Suddenly Vlad was bouncing up and down like a bee caught in a wind tunnel. His beady eyes blazed fury, though. "You're making this more difficult than it has to be, Daniel."

Hawk and bat stared intently, sizing each other up, looking for an opening.

I didn't know if Vlad was a fan of Westerns, but the silence reminded me of the tension at the O.K. Corral just before the big gunfight erupts. All we needed was tumbleweed bouncing across the street between us and the scene would have been complete.

Finally Vlad's mouth opened in a snarl. "Daniel, you've made your last mistake. Now your friends will suffer before I —"

"Oh, shut up," I said.

And then, I leaned forward, gave a swift peck with my beak — *and ate him!*

Chapter 25

YOU THINK *you're* disgusted—how about me?

I just ate a batwich.

Alien Hunters must use whatever means necessary to catch their prey, though. And, after all, birds eat bats. Vlad had disappeared into my hooked beak in only a couple of gulps—snapped up like one of those "sliders," the mini-burgers they serve at White Castle—almost before I knew what I was doing. And that was that. He was gone.

Have you ever been out running or riding a bike and accidentally eaten a bug? Well, this was that, times about a thousand. I had returned to my normal human shape a second later, and I was coughing and retching, my tongue sticking out. I wish I could say bats taste like chicken. They don't, unless maybe you count raw chicken that's been left out in the sun for a few centuries.

At this point, I suddenly realized that *everyone* in the room was frozen, staring at me. The other vampires looked more than a little nervous at the way the dinner table had just been turned. And my friends just looked — *grossed out*. Okay, they also looked like they were holding in wild howls of laughter that would have filled the room and spilled out onto the street, but disgust was definitely their main sentiment.

Joe kindly broke the silence: "Now, that was a lesson in biology you wouldn't want to see on the Discovery Channel."

I knew *Vampirus sapiens* traveled in packs, led by an alpha male. It seemed clear that they'd been under Vlad's alpha spell for a long, long time. Now that they were free again, I could see that they were flooded with feelings that they hadn't experienced in decades, if not centuries.

Fear, for example. And confusion. The minion holding Joe was making a face like he'd just wet his pants.

I decided to take advantage of it. "Well?" I said threateningly. "Is anybody else interested in a little brain sucking? Or are we done here?"

There was a mad rush for the windows, then a flurry of bodies and wings hurling themselves into the dark night. Only then did I collapse onto the floor and begin to shake like a leaf.

"Daniel, you've got to stop bringing your work home with you," Emma recommended.

I sighed. "Believe me, I would if I could." *But with Vlad threatening my friends with instant death,* I thought, *he might as well have hung a sign around his neck that said* BLUE PLATE SPECIAL.

PART TWO
YOU WON'T GUESS WHERE THIS IS HEADING . . .

Chapter 26

THREE HOURS LATER, I still couldn't bring myself to sleep. I'd gotten up six, maybe seven times to brush my teeth and gargle with some full-strength, *yellow* Listerine mouthwash I'd found. Even that nasty stuff didn't help.

I was sitting on a sofa by myself, staring moodily into the empty fireplace. Fear and loathing were eating away at me, and let me tell you they were taking huge mouthfuls.

More and more I was finding myself unable to use my powers when I'd wanted to or needed to. Sure, little things were working (mirror, check; explosive, check), and one superbig thing had worked—the hawk—but only after I'd failed on several other attempts.

What was going on? *Was this feeling ever going to stop? When?*

"When you let it."

I jumped, even though the voice was familiar. Well, more than familiar—it belonged to my father. My dad came strolling into the room from the hallway with his hands in his pockets like it was the most natural thing in the world. It was the first time I'd ever experienced my dad—or the ghost of him, or whatever he was—manifesting himself in full-body form without my help.

"Don't do that!" I exclaimed.

"Do what?" Dad said innocently enough. "Look, Daniel, you've had too many close calls recently." I didn't say anything—I didn't know what to say—and he went on. "You're working your way up The List. Things are getting much more dangerous. I'm here because you obviously need a little help."

"How?" I asked him. My father, my real father, had died in Kansas twelve years ago. The dad standing next to me could talk, he could comfort me, but to help fight—

"You're right," he said, interrupting—no, *answering* my train of thought. "I can't fight your battles. But I can still help. I'm going to help you help yourself. You've got tremendous power inside you, Daniel. Many times the power your mother and I had. I'm going to train you to be what I never was."

Before I even got in a "gee, thanks, Dad," my father stuck his hand in my face and barked like a drill sergeant. So much for unconditional love and warm fuzzies.

"This *isn't* going to be a walk in the park, so *don't* smile! In fact, *don't even think about smiling!* This is going to be the most *difficult* hour of your life! And that'll be *nothing* compared to *the second hour!* Now follow me!"

I wanted to roll my eyes, but instead I dressed quickly and followed my father to the front door. And that's when I gulped.

Instead of the dingy, cluttered sidewalk of D'Arblay Street, a wide, rocky beach stretched out beyond the doorsill. Farther away was a darkness that somehow I just knew was the ocean.

And here was the part that really got me: over the horizon, *three purplish crescent moons hung in the sky.*

Chapter 27

OVERALL, the whole place looked like something puked up by a mountain. And it was hot. Eating-five-alarm-chili-while-locked-in-a-sauna hot.

The landscape before me was alien — and I mean that quite literally. I'd seen pictures of lava flows in Hawaii, black rock twisted into undulating formations that looked almost alive. What I was looking at was like that, crossed with a bunch of moshers at a punk concert. Spiky rocks jutted up everywhere, ten, twenty feet high. Every edge glistened in the moonlight.

I turned to look behind me, but the door I'd

just come through was gone. The whole building had vanished. There were only rocks as far
as my eye could see.

My father started running toward the shore
in a curious zigzag, jumping and weaving like he
was in a video game, until he was on the other
side of the beach, standing on a spiny black ridge
next to the water.

His voice was faint. "Come over here! And,
Daniel...stay on the path."

What path? I tried to visualize where he'd
stepped. No dice.

Oh well. Here goes nothing.

I took a deep breath and made a running
jump in what I hoped was the right direction.
I landed near the top of one of the tall, jagged
spires and balanced on one foot for a moment,
trying to figure out where to jump next. But no
sooner had my foot touched the rock than I felt
the surface lurch sickeningly beneath me.

When I looked down, I saw smoke. A second
later, the smell of burning rubber reached my
nose. The rock was so hot that the soles of my
shoes were melting.

Barely thinking, I jumped down to one of the lower rock humps. And then I got another surprise. This time, it was the ground that was moving.

Beneath me, the four-foot-wide hump yawned open like a mouth to reveal a gaping pit with jagged glass walls. It was like a laundry chute direct to the underworld, and I was spread-eagled right over it. "Uh, Dad?"

"I told you to stick to the path."

"This isn't exactly fair!" I gasped, trying to keep myself above the ground somehow.

"You think Phosphorius Beta will play fair? You think The Prayer will? *None of them ever do.* Look at what happened to me! Ambushed in my own house when your mom and I were cooking potpies."

I gathered all of my strength into my legs and hurled myself forward. The rocks below me snapped shut, the rough sides rubbing against one another sounding like bones being ground to powder.

I landed on one of the jagged peaks but quickly felt myself slipping. My arms were still windmilling as my body tilted backward and my feet flew up in the air. In a second I would land in a pit of sharp, grinding stone and turn into filling for a nice English mincemeat pie.

That was it. If my father wasn't going to play fair, neither was I.

Chapter 28

IN THE BLINK OF AN EYE I aimed a mental bolt downward in a straight line, and felt carbon fibers wrap themselves around one another, traveling faster than thought.

Now I was holding a flexible rod, sixteen feet long, Olympic-standard size and weight for pole vaulting. And while I was still in midair, I spun around and stuck it in the crevice between two chomping rock pits, using my momentum and the pole's pliancy to carry me up and over another of the tall rock formations.

At the peak of my arc, I dropped the pole and threw my hands up, grasping at something that till that moment had existed only in my head: a makeshift parasail. It wasn't exactly elegant, but the rough, thin strands of rope attached to the corners of a square canvas sheet would get the job done.

I couldn't help letting out a whoop of excitement as I glided over the entire bizarre-o landscape and landed lightly beside my father.

And people thought skateboarding was an extreme sport?

"Well, how was that, Dad?"

"Hmph." I could see he was trying to contain a smile. "I brought you here to teach you to pay attention to your surroundings. Creativity is your strength, but it isn't everything. You can't imagine your way out of *every* situation." He paused a moment, looking me right in the eye. "Take it from me."

"Well, speaking of surroundings, what is this place?"

"Cyndaris," Dad replied. "Beta's home planet."

"But I thought—"

"That it was too hot to support life? That's

mostly true. We're at Cyndaris's North Pole, the coldest place on the entire planet. A few miles in any direction, and you would burn up faster than a firecracker on the Fourth of July."

The triple moons hung low over the "ocean" (which I realized now couldn't be water, not in this heat), tinting it violet. The List had mentioned that some of Beta's people were cultured, even poetic, and, minus the whole burning-everything-in-sight side of things, I could see where they might draw some of their artistic inspiration. I had to admit the view was amazing.

"What's with the rocks?"

"Carbon-based life never evolved here. These rocks are living organisms. Carnivorous ones. Think of them as Cyndarian flytraps. They generate heat to attract fire-based life. Then swallow it whole."

The perfect setting for Dad's boot camp.

Chapter 29

AN HOUR LATER, every muscle in my body was aching. Even my teeth hurt.

Training with Dad sure wasn't like watching *The Karate Kid*. This was the furthest thing from martial arts training, or learning to turn myself into a mosquito or an elephant or learning to whip up a stun gun right in front of a nasty alien beastie. Instead, this training consisted of paddling out to a rock in a dinghy (through some kind of toxic liquid that can actually exist in these temperatures), carrying the dinghy to the other side of the beach, and then starting all over again.

I'd done close to thirty runs back and forth over the deadly beach, balancing the dinghy with my hands and head as I tried to figure out a safe path among the hungry stone jaws. I have to say, I was getting pretty darn good at it. Only problem was, I was getting tired. It was hard to think. I wouldn't be able to create another vaulting pole. I doubted I could create a drinking straw.

Then, on my thirty-second trip back to the water, I fell. There was no rock within reach. I watched helplessly as the boat toppled out of my grasp and was chewed to pieces by one of the waiting mouths below. Meanwhile, I was about to be impaled by a stone hotter than a stovetop. I gritted my teeth and tightened my chest as much as I could in preparation for impact.

And then something happened that had happened to me only once before.

Time stopped.

Chapter 30

MY BODY WAS FROZEN about six inches away from a searing hot, pointy rock. The crunching sounds that had become nearly constant were silenced, as was the lapping of the waves on the shore.

"Well, watching you work so hard has been great fun," my father said, leaning closer to me. "But I guess we should really come to the point of tonight's lesson."

Not a minute too soon, I wanted to say, but my lips couldn't move. Neither could my head, so I could just barely see Dad in my peripheral vision. *Couldn't we have skipped the basic training and just gotten to the point?*

"I know this ability to manipulate time is something we went over quite awhile ago, you and I. But it's only now that you're grown up that some of the potential that your mother and I saw in you is finally being unlocked. So there are a few things you should know."

He stood up taller, his voice becoming more military again. "Number one: bringing new things into the world is not an ability you should take lightly. But being able to go back and change things is an even greater burden." He sighed. "I was never too good at it. None of the family was. So frankly we don't know much about what effect it might have on the universe as a whole. All we know is that it puts a tremendous strain on your body and mind. *So be careful, and don't abuse the power, Daniel.*

"Number two: time travel. It's not an easy power to use. Believe me, I've tried. When The Prayer went after your mother..." His voice trailed off for a moment, and I was almost glad I couldn't see his expression. "Short story is, time travel seems to be connected to emotion. It can be triggered only when you are feeling something, and feeling it very strongly."

That must be how I did it before, in the van.

"Number three: powerful events can create 'stress points' in time. What I mean is, they pretty much punch a hole right in the time stream. It's always been said that a powerful enough Alien Hunter can not only find these holes, but can actually travel between them. I believe that you can, Daniel. You just need to figure out how."

He sighed again. "Daniel, you carried yourself well tonight. I'd say you're at least one percent—okay, okay, maybe one and a quarter percent—of the way to being a truly effective Alien Hunter."

Fantastic. I really wished I could groan. And then something struck me. If time is stopped, how come—

My father answered before I'd even finished the thought. "How come I'm not frozen? How should I know? This is your dream."

Dream?

As if on cue, time started again. I felt the air pop in my ears, and a split second later I felt an object hit my sternum with the force of a red-hot sledgehammer.

Chapter 31

EVEN THOUGH it was "just a dream," I took off the entire next day. Facing blazing fireballs and ferocious brain suckers was enough work for twenty-four hours.

Strangely, the burn mark on my chest from that fiery eyeball looked even worse now—the red marks sorta looked like a face howling with laughter—and I wondered if the training session hadn't been real. In another dimension.

I treated my friends to a matinee performance at Shakespeare's Globe Theatre. It's a giant circular arena with a thatched roof, and it's where Shakespeare's plays were originally performed. If you get to London, or if you *live* in London, you have to check it out.

The play was *The Tempest,* about a magician called Prospero who lives with his daughter on an island. What really got me was, at the end Prospero gives up his powers, throwing his spell book into the sea. In a lot of ways, I majorly *envied* the guy.

But then: What would my life be like if I just gave up the mission? The List?

I don't think I could exist without it.

By the way, this is exactly what my little break from hunting Beta felt like—a single page in a book.

Chapter 32

A LITTLE TIME OFF was good, and it had been very necessary. But this was where I really felt at home: stalking my prey.

The last glimmers of the setting sun glinted off one of the cracked fifth-floor windows in the dingy apartment building, dazzling me a little. I was hiding on the opposite roof, watching The Cockney Fireman (as Joe had started calling him).

At six fifty-two, I saw the guy emerge from the front door of his building. He glanced furtively around the cul-de-sac through his aviator sunglasses, spat some foul goo onto the street, and strode off purposefully with a strange lop-sided gait. He was headed to the main road. And I had someone already waiting for him.

"He just passed me," said Willy in my head. "I'm sticking to The Cockney Fireman like peanut butter on the roof of your mouth. If he's meeting with Beta, you'll be the first to know."

"All right. Divide and conquer. But, Willy, be extra careful," I said. Willy would tail the creep wherever he was headed, giving me the chance to search his apartment.

I immediately scrambled across the tiled roofs surrounding the alley until I was on top of The Fireman's building. Then I dropped down onto the top level of the fire escape. It was slick and rickety, and I made my way carefully, then down the rusted ladder to the third floor.

Behind a filthy window, the apartment was full of shadows. I created a thin crowbar and jimmied the window open, trying not to make a sound.

As I slid it up, a medley of truly foul smells drifted out, almost knocking me backward. As messy as the place was, it smelled a hundred times worse: gasoline, sweat, vinegar, unwashed socks and underwear, all mixing into a rancid cocktail.

I did *not* want to go in there.

Of course, I had to: with The Cockney Fireman out of the way for a while, now was my chance to see what else he was hiding besides the cases of motor oil that he drank like diet colas.

"Like what he's done with the place," I mumbled to myself. "Wonder who his decorator is? The Tasmanian Devil?"

The disgusting kitchen was connected to an equally foul-smelling living room. A brown fabric couch, covered with singe marks and empty oil cans, dominated the place. The TV looked as if it had broken long ago: a fist-sized hole was smashed in the screen; a Wolverhampton Wanderers soccer jersey lay on top, discarded, its arms missing.

I swallowed hard. The sleeves looked like they had been burned off. I wondered whose jersey it had been—and whether or not the dude still had his arms.

Then I heard something. A soft, muffled

whimpering coming from behind a closed door next to the couch. A trap?

No—the notes of fear, of hopelessness, sounded too genuine to me. *They were the same sort of terrified sounds I had made the night my parents died.*

In less than a second, I moved to the door and threw it open—revealing a dank bedroom, illuminated by a dim, flickering light. There was definitely a theme going on in this place decorwise. Soiled, bare mattress? *Check.* Mounds of trash? *Check.* Trembling little girl? *Big check.*

She was seven or eight at most, lots of brown curls, her face as pale as paper. She whimpered pitifully as I entered the room.

"Don't worry, sweetie. I'm not going to hurt you," I said in a quiet voice. "I'm going to get you out of here. I'm Daniel. What's your name?"

"Su-san," she said. And then she choked out, "I want to go home! Please, please!" before bursting into tears that brought some to my own eyes.

I dug around in my pocket for some tissues before giving up and simply creating a handkerchief. When I knelt down to hand it to her, I realized she'd stopped crying. She was staring over my shoulder. Then she raised a hand to point behind me.

I turned slowly.

It was him, The Cockney Fireman, sunglasses off, teeth bared, flames seeping from both nostrils and one eye.

"'Ello, mate. Back to try a little of me home cookin'?"

Bad, bad news, but what was worse —

Willy had promised to let me know the creep's whereabouts.

So what happened to Willy?

Chapter 33

NORMALLY, I would have flexed right into a defensive stance. But something nearly uncontrollable inside was pushing me toward the offense this time. I leaned toward him fearlessly.

"If you did anything to hurt my friend, I swear I'll *extinguish* you," I hissed.

"Oi dunna what yer talkin' about." He grimaced. "Huh! Beta didn't tell me yah were a nutter."

The flame in his nostrils and eye flared a little, then came out his ears, too. "Oi thought yah would have realoized after our last meetin' just how dangerous a game yer playin'." He shrugged. "But Oi guess Oi'm gonna get to kill ya after all. *Good-ee.*"

His face had begun to distort before he'd even finished, and now a ball of fire burst from his bad eye—good eye?—aimed straight for my heart.

Instantly I focused on the physical space in front of me and watched the fireball dissolve before it got close enough to even singe my shirt.

"What the—" growled Beta's henchman, loosing another three bursts of flame. They, too, died in midair.

Just because I can create things doesn't mean they always have to be *visible.* In this case, my defense screen was something neither of us could see, a concentrated cloud of carbon dioxide. It's basic chemistry: no oxygen, no fire. No fire, no burned-to-a-crisp Daniel.

He frowned. "So, you've figured out 'ow to put out my foire. Well played, mate. It's toime to get out the big guns, then."

The Fireman had turned his head upward and raised his hands in front of him, like he was waiting for it to start raining fire.

Then, out of nowhere, his mouth opened and he gave a bloodcurdling, unearthly scream. *The scream of a man being burned alive,* I couldn't help thinking. A moment later, the sleeves of his denim jacket burst into flame. They were burned away in an instant, and I could see his massive arms, glowing a dull, angry red, the color of molten metal.

And then—oh, crap—*I saw the volcanoes!*

Around the room, on all four walls, the ceiling, and the floor, miniature craters were appearing, blackened rings rising from the plaster, the wood paneling, the rug.

The room took on a reddish glow, and from the center of each crater, lava began to flow, first in drops, then in rivers from the ceiling, down the walls, flowing and pooling on the floor.

The heat was unbearable. What with The Fireman's screaming, it probably wasn't that different from hell.

Or maybe this room was a branch office?

Chapter 34

STEAMING LAVA already covered most of the floor. In less than a minute, there would be nowhere left to stand without getting severely scalded. I was blanketing my body as best I could with carbon dioxide, but there was no way I could keep up with this much fire.

The only area left untouched was a small circle where The Fireman stood. If I wanted to get out of here without turning into a pile of charcoal briquettes, that was my only chance.

He finally stopped screaming and lowered his head to look at me — just as I did a flying leap and tackled him into a bubbling pool of lava.

I was using his body to shield myself from the red-hot liquid.

There was a loud *sizzle,* but he didn't cry out. Suddenly his skin radiated heat like a house on fire. Even when my hands started blistering, I didn't let go.

He was grunting between gritted teeth, and squinting at me through smoke-clouded eyes. Then his panting and grunting took on a different tone, a deep, vicious crackle.

A moment later there was a searing explosion and his body burst into flame.

Just in time, I jumped back into the clear area in the middle of the floor. In seconds, there was nothing left of him, only flames.

But they were getting higher and higher. And hotter.

What was going on?

I put my hand to my face to shield myself, and that's when I heard a voice. Not a cockney one. A voice like the roar of a rocket lifting off. There's a biblical story about Moses in the desert, talking to the burning bush. It couldn't have sounded much different from this.

"So this is the fly in the ointment, is it? The infamous Alien Hunter, Daniel X."

The Cockney Fireman was gone. In front of me was a fiery blossom rising right out of the lava on the floor. Directly in the center, between its flaming petals, a dark maw yawned like one of the rock pits I had seen during the training session with my father. That was where the voice came from.

"Phosphorius Beta, I presume."

Chapter 35

THE FLAMES all around him flickered green, then purple, and then a brighter red than I had ever seen. It might have been beautiful if I didn't know that he was the third deadliest alien on the planet.

"I would congratulate you on your perceptiveness, but you're not worthy to even speak my name. I have been doing business here a long, long time. This is *my* country. Was always meant to be. And you and your bloody friends went and messed with it."

I narrowed my eyes. "What happened to the Cockney? Your hotshot henchman?"

"My 'hotshot henchman'? *Ha!* You're funny, aren't you?" The fire flared up in what might have been a laugh. "He's gone, punk. All burned up. I've been in business far too long to put up with failure like his. And I've been hunting you down for far too long not to get my revenge at last."

I had no idea what he was talking about but wouldn't let myself get distracted by his babble. The lava had cooled quickly, and as he spoke I began edging my way toward the balcony door, toeing slowly to find a solid path. The heat coming from Beta was intense, and it unnerved me more than I'd like to admit. Even with all of my father's training, fire took me back to the most traumatic event of my life.

"What do you need *her* for?" I indicated the bedroom door with my thumb. The distraction technique again. If he got close enough to touch me, no amount of carbon dioxide would save me from being charbroiled.

"Susan? That little cipher? She's just fuel for the fire. As impure as the humans are, I find their physical forms *can* be useful, from time to time."

"You're quite the sensitive chap, aren't you," I said sarcastically. "I just get such a good feeling about you, you know?"

"Sensitivity is for those who are accustomed to losing. Like you."

At last, I felt the concrete of the balcony beneath my feet. Beta seemed to notice I was moving, and his fire jumped halfway across the room. Its petals blasted heat in my direction, and his voice held an extra note of menace.

"Going somewhere? Or maybe you prefer death by falling over death by being burned alive?"

I backed up all the way to the railing and closed my hand around it. As I expected, it felt flimsy, much like the one on the fire escape.

Beta's fire whooshed across the floor and re-formed at the balcony door—a roaring pillar that singed the top of the doorframe. Something like a dark face was visible under its surface, but it was flickering so violently I couldn't be sure.

The column spun, unleashing a howl of air that formed speech. "End of the line, Daniel. Any last words? Reflections on our great times together?"

"Sure," I began. The memory of a fire at a Kansas farmhouse so many years ago sent a pang of terror through me for a millisecond before I pushed through it. "How 'bout 'You're not as hot as you think you are!'?"

As the flames rushed forward, I kicked backward with my foot, knocking the railing away. Then I let myself fall.

At the last possible second, I grabbed the edge of the balcony, my legs dangling high over the courtyard.

Beta rushed at the space where I had been a moment ago. He passed right over my head. As he swept over my fingers I felt a searing pain, but I held the concrete ledge with a death grip.

I turned to watch him fall off the balcony, toward a dirty swimming pool below.

Beta looked like a writhing, burning meteor as he descended. Tongues of flame licked upward, but he was falling too fast to burn me.

"I'll see you again soon, Alien Hunter. You have no hope of winning. There are too many of us! Too many..."

A splash and a hiss drowned out whatever

Beta said next. The whole courtyard was suddenly full of steam.

My hands were raw and blistered, but I held on to the balcony and peered down into the courtyard. The pool was half-empty now — and there was no trace of fire, or Beta.

Too many of us? What the heck did that mean?

Chapter 36

MY CLOTHES WERE BURNED, my hands were badly blistered, and I smelled like I had been wrestling charred hogs in a barbecue pit. Susan didn't seem to mind, though. As soon as I opened up the bedroom door the little girl ran out and gave me a big hug. It was painful, but I didn't care. Saving someone always feels good.

"Is the bad man gone?" she whispered. "Is he?"

"Yes. He's gone, Susan. He'll never come back. You're safe."

"But are *you* safe?" the little girl said to me.

And then, a big oops. Major oops. I realized

part of what my father had been trying to prepare me for.

Suddenly the little girl's shape before me was like a Venus flytrap with hundreds of legs and arms. And she was shrieking at me: "YOU MURDERED HIM, MURDERED HIM, MURDERED MY FIREMAN!"

Flames shot out at me, and the heat was unbearable. Worse still, the little monster was blocking both the doorway and the room's only window.

Moth—it was the odd thought in my brain, the only small possibility that I might live through this new sneak attack.

So like a moth, *I went right into the flames,* and I grabbed the core with all my remaining strength.

"MURDERER! TAKE YOUR HANDS OFF ME!" it continued to scream. "MURDERER, LET GO!"

But I wouldn't let go and I wouldn't stop charging straight ahead either.

"Come with me, Susan!"

I crashed through the window with the

blazing, squealing creature in my arms. Then I was falling, falling, falling.

And then... I was swimming in the remains of the pool down in the courtyard.

And my attacker was nothing but hot air.

Too many of us, Beta had said.

And Susan had been one of them.

Chapter 37

EVERYTHING AFTER THAT quickly went from bad to worse. When I got back to the town house, Willy hadn't returned, and there was no clue as to what had happened to him after he began to follow The Cockney Fireman.

I didn't need a clue. There was no question in my mind that Beta or one of his minions had been up to no good. This time when I stormed out to find answers, I refused to let any of my friends come along. I bear-hugged Joe and Dana, and I promised the tear-streaked Emma that I would not come back without Willy.

I could not, would not, ever lose one of my friends again.

The sign outside B. Faust and Company, Ltd., said the shop closed at seven. But now it was eight thirty and there was still an eerily bright glow seeping through the cracks around the metal shutters that covered the entrance.

I climbed a fence and from there hoisted myself up a drainpipe to the roof. When Emma and I had last visited, I'd noticed skylights. Time to see if they might give me an easy way inside.

There. Three skylights, in a neat row. I could hear voices, so I crept up on hands and knees as silently as I could. All three skylights were opaque with soot and grime, but one was missing a pane in the corner. A dim golden light was flickering inside.

Cautiously, I put my face to the hole. From my vantage point I could see the whole room, and let me tell you, it wasn't a pretty sight.

The place hadn't shut down at all. About a dozen "people" were still scurrying around, wheeling tubs of molten metal or manipulating unfamiliar objects glowing with heat. *What* they were making, I had no idea. *How* they were making it . . . well, that was the really freaky part.

One enormously muscular man was welding two curved metal plates together. He was being showered in sparks but wasn't wearing a mask. "Safety first" didn't really seem to be a major issue in this place, though, because he didn't even have a welder. He was just *running his finger* up and down the join between the plates, while a white-hot scalpel of flame extended above his fingernail like an extra knuckle, searing the pieces in place.

A few yards away from him, another man with a tumorous paunch held a thick metal bar in front of him like bicycle handlebars. As I watched, the metal began to turn red between his hands, until the whole center of the bar was glowing. Then, as gently as if he were stroking a cat, he massaged it into a smooth curve and tossed it onto a pile of similar pieces.

Everyone in the workshop had the same fire-scarred hands that I'd seen on The Cockney Fireman. And they all looked withered somehow, like the life had been sucked out of them . . .

like the only thing keeping them alive was gasoline and spark plugs.

There was a movement just below me, and I looked down. Separated from the rest of the workers by a partition was a little break room, complete with microwave, sink, and a small stovetop encrusted with old food.

The grizzled, unpleasant woman who had yelled at Emma and me two days before was sitting at a rickety table with a cup of tea in front of her, tapping one foot against the other nervously, like she was waiting for someone.

Or *something*.

A sound made her jump a little, and her head turned toward the stove. All four of the burners on the range had lit on their own and were burning with orange flames that extended at least six inches in the air.

In a matter of seconds, the flames grew even higher, and came together, until they formed a giant ball of fire that hung over the stove like a miniature sun.

Then, almost daintily, the flames stepped

down onto the cement floor, burning in a flaming blossom that was all too familiar to me.

This was the same flaming monster that I'd drowned in a dirty apartment swimming pool.

Beta was back in all his glory!

Chapter 38

AT BETA'S APPEARANCE, the woman jumped up so fast she knocked over her chair, and she turned her head away. The monster was so bright that it was hard to look at directly.

"It's you!" she cried out in a gasp. "They told me you would come for me."

"Yesssssssssss," came the hiss. "Are you prepared for me, dearheart? Are you prepared to receive my power?"

Her voice rasped eagerly. "Yes, yes. Make me one of your flame weavers. I want to know what it feels like to have fire at my fingertips. To have fire within me. To be…"

"To be something more than what you are?" The tongues of flame were waggling with suppressed laughter. "Very well, *ask and ye shall receive.*"

All of a sudden, Beta flared till he towered over the grim-faced woman. Her docile smile faded and she took a step back. An instant later, she was enveloped in flame as Beta poured over her like a deluge.

I couldn't even see her anymore. But I could hear her. Her voice had lost its eagerness. "It... it burns. Is it supposed to — no, no!... I want it to stop! I —"

She gave a shriek that made my skin prickle, but no one in the rest of the workshop even looked up. And then it was over.

All that was left of Beta was a wisp of flame flickering from the woman's mouth, which she quickly sucked inside like a long strand of spaghetti.

Her fear was gone, replaced by a bland, satisfied smile. Her eyes glistened, but they were strangely hollow. It was like the lights were on, but nobody was home. She smiled mechanically, but believe me when I say that her face was the type that should never smile.

"More drones for the hive," she said in a voice that was raspier and scarier than ever. Then she strode off to join the rest of the staff on the workshop floor. "Woman's work is never done," she muttered.

Chapter 39

AN HOUR LATER, I'd gotten no more answers or any glimpses of Willy. And what Beta had said at the apartment building was still bothering me. *Too many of us.* There might be a handful of surly-looking goons here—sorry, flame weavers—but he'd made it sound like he had a dangerous personal army.

The answer was clear to me: B. Faust might be Beta's factory, but it wasn't his official headquarters. Not even close.

Finally I saw two of the workers leaving the factory floor, the grizzled woman and a tall, balding man who looked like he could be Homer

Simpson's brother. Between them was a wheel-barrow hauling a huge bin full of parts. They took it out through a back door.

I crawled across the roof to watch as they emerged behind the building and began lifting the pieces into an unmarked, coal-black delivery truck backed up to a loading dock.

When they took the wheelbarrow back inside, I let myself down onto the roof of the truck, then onto its cargo bay. I didn't know where they were taking this stuff, but I wanted to find out as much as I could about it.

It wouldn't be long before they came back with another load, and there wasn't anywhere to hide unless I felt like being crushed under two tons of steel.

Well, wait a minute. Maybe that wasn't such a terrible idea.

I sat on top of the pile, pulled my legs up to my chest, and closed my eyes, feeling the cold, hard metal beneath me, the way the iron molecules stacked and nested in one another like oranges jammed into a crate. It was a particularly difficult morph, but I was stoked and motivated with real anger at Beta now, and a few seconds later, I clattered to the floor of the cargo bay. I'd changed myself. I was now a curved steel bar on the top of a pile of similar pieces.

Minutes later, the flame weavers returned and dumped another cartload of parts into the truck — right on top of me.

"Let's get going," said the male in a low growl. "He's expecting these for tonight. We do not want to disappoint Phosphorius Beta."

Chapter 40

THE CLANKING OF METAL was deafening. Going to an AC/DC concert would have been more relaxing than riding in the back of this truck. I'm no librarian, but after a while the enforced, cocoonlike silence of a reading room was starting to seem attractive.

The truck made three stops, and at each one I felt more parts being dumped on top of me. If I hadn't been made of manganese steel, the same thing they make bulldozer blades out of, I would have been as flat as a pancake by now.

I don't know how far we went. Maybe fifty miles or more. It was quiet and dark for a long while in the back of the truck, and then suddenly we were surrounded by clanking, bustling, crackling sounds that got louder and louder and *louder.* It sounded like we were riding an elevator into a mineshaft that was traveling deep into the bowels of the earth.

We stopped about halfway to China, it seemed, and the cargo bay's rolling door opened with a clatter. Voices and stomping feet filled the truck, and I was picked up and flung through the air.

"'Bout time you got here," I heard a deep voice say. "Tonight's the big night."

Chapter 41

WHEN I WAS AWAY from the main source of the light, I changed back to my regular form, and — bang! — promptly smacked my head on something.

It turned out I was crammed into an industrial-sized washing machine that was big enough to hold me and all the metal keeping me company, but not by much. The walls of the washtub were discolored and spotted with rust.

There was an overpoweringly rancid smell in the air and, breathing through my mouth, I shrank back as best I could and took a peek out through the machine's door. I *wasn't* underground, as I'd thought.

And I didn't like what I saw. For miles, it seemed, the landscape was made up entirely of piles and piles of trash, with hundreds of human silhouettes moving among them. On the piles burned thousands of fires, all swaying with the same terrible rhythm, as if under the control of a single beating heart. Suddenly I knew what I was up against, something I could never hope to beat.

Now I knew what Beta had meant by "too many of us." The evil spawning here seemed infinite. *There could be a million of him at this dump alone.*

If things keep going this way, I'm gonna be toast before long, I thought. Burnt black and to a crisp, smoking like a chimney.

With perfect timing, the universe — or maybe it was my father, or maybe it was Beta — decided to play a cruel joke on me. Regardless, I knew that when I got around to telling this story someday, Joe would say it was a *really* good one.

Because right at that minute, the washing machine turned on.

And I was about to be smashed to pieces.

Chapter 42

WELL, if this adventure didn't get me an alien, I would at least come out of it brand-spankin'-clean, I thought, silently slumping down in the barrel of the washing machine.

As it turns out, my potential bloodbath was more like a nuclear-powered water massage than a spin in a clothing washer full of metal bars. A regular human probably wouldn't have survived the pressure, but Alparians have a pretty tough hide.

I heard voices approaching and didn't waste a second before I focused entirely on returning to bar form. It wasn't long before three flame weavers in overalls opened the machine door and began loading the metal pieces into what looked like a mine cart that ran on rails.

They had barely started, though, when I heard a massive, roaring boom sweep through the dump, shaking the ground so much that some of the workers actually fell over like tenpins after a strike in bowling. I could see human figures running through thousands of fires toward the highest piles of garbage.

Now was my chance! I rolled out of the machine and across the shadowy aisle between two rows of stacked tires. The ground was still trembling, so no one would find it odd that something was skittering across the ground toward the site of the explosion.

At least I thought no one would notice. I was wrong.

One worker (I couldn't make out if it was male or female as I rolled faster and faster in the dim light) was far more interested in an errant piece of metal than in the freaking *earthquake* that seemed to be going on.

Maintaining bar form was hard enough, but

rolling at top speed on top of that? Dizzyingly exhausting. After the world's weirdest mini chase scene, I felt the worker's hand swipe me from the ground just as I heard the voice.

"You dumb piece of junk!" she grumbled. "Relax. It's Dana."

Chapter 43

YOU KNOW how crazy I am about Dana? Enough to actually charge a rod of metal with emotion. Just in case you thought inanimate objects have no emotions, think again.

I wanted to kill her and hug her at the same time. As I was still a rod, I couldn't do either one. She dashed with me in hand to the other side of a junked car—a French make called a Peugeot—and pried the door open. She slid into the backseat, where I returned to human form.

"You weren't supposed to come with me," was the first thing out of my mouth. "This is way too dangerous, Dana. And *how* did you—I mean, I didn't—"

"We'll talk about it later, Daniel. Something big is about to happen." She edged up to the opposite window to get a better view of the madness, and I followed. Now we were looking out on a circle cleared in the middle of the garbage, a circle as wide as a football field.

Opposite where we were, the ground dropped away, and I was surprised to see the ocean on the other side; we were on the coast somewhere.

In the middle of this improvised stadium of trash was a gigantic misshapen metal structure that looked like the result of a fight between a giant squid and a monster truck. It was the source of the vibrations that were shaking everything for a mile around.

I recognized it instantly. I'd read its description many times in The List's file on Beta. The multitentacled monster before me was a Cyndarian spaceship.

Suddenly the vibrations became even more powerful. It looked like it was ready for takeoff.

Bits of garbage began to topple from the piles,

and the Peugeot was rained on by ash, pieces of plastic, rusty circuit boards. The ship tried to lift off, but for some reason it couldn't. The force of the flames pushing through its own rockets was literally tearing it apart.

There was a horrendous sound like Godzilla scraping his nails on a chalkboard, and the ship actually keeled to one side. The crowds shied away now, drawing back into the shelter of the trash piles.

And then there was a shattering explosion, like nothing I'd ever heard before. Blue flames, blowing gaping holes in the sides of the spaceship, shot into the air about a half mile.

When the smoke cleared, I could still see the ship, looking more like a used firecracker now. And pouring out of hundreds of holes was its cargo.

The "fuel" that Beta was sending home wasn't oil, or coal, it turned out. It was, well, everything I loved about Terra Firma, stuffed into a cold metal container. Lush green trees, with their trunks, leaves, branches, spilled out onto the ground. Mixed in were what must have been hundreds of tons of flowers, bushes, grasses of all kinds.

And then I saw the passengers.

I could see rows of cages, with animals of all kinds imprisoned inside — dogs, cats, chickens, rabbits, foxes, horses. And then there was a cacophony of sound coming from inside the damaged metal shell. Flocks of birds flew out of one hole, where the vibrations had shaken open some cage doors. The birds circled the ship, squawking in the air.

I clenched my fists in fury. Inside that ship was a nature documentary's worth of plants and animals, and it was abundantly clear what Beta wanted with them. All of the wonderful life that Earth had to offer was nothing more to him than *fuel*.

Chapter 44

THE GHOSTLY FLAMES from the burning piles had gathered, risen, and snaked around the dump to witness the collapse. Now they roared high into the air, and burst apart into hundreds of smaller flames that darted around the base of the broken ship.

Then a rustling, crackling voice swept through the dump.

"The Alien Hunter is here. He is close by. Find him. NOW! BRING HIM TO ME DEAD OR ALIVE! WHOEVER BRINGS ME DANIEL X WILL GLOW FOR ETERNITY!"

The workers scattered at the command,

fanning out through the narrow aisles of the dump.

"See why you needed me here, Daniel?" Dana said.

"No," I told her angrily. "This is about me, not you."

"I'm part of you. We're a part of each other. It's all the same."

"Just...disappear, Dana! Disappear!"

We'd wasted precious moments with our argument, because Beta had embarked on his own search. I guess he wanted to glow for eternity, too.

His flames had abandoned ship and spread through the dump, each fire stream covering more ground in a few seconds than a human could in an hour.

"Okay, Daniel," said Dana. "This is the part where you disappear us and then, like, create a rainstorm or something major to take out this maniac."

"Got it."

But I couldn't. I tried, and tried again.

I wanted to howl with frustration. I'd just gone metal a few times like it was nothing.

I didn't have time for a Plan B before we heard a knocking at the window. We hunched down in the car's backseat, trying to make ourselves as invisible as possible, but we couldn't escape Beta's voice.

"I know you're in there, Dan—Dana—Daniel...*come out, come out, whoever you are!*"

When I looked up, all I could see were rainbows of fire: orange, yellow, green, red, covering every window, enveloping the entire car.

Chapter 45

SO I GUESS YOU'D CALL THIS a really bad emergency situation. A mind-and-body blower.

Right in front of me, hovering outside the rear window, was an indistinct shadow in the middle of the flames—like a face. The Dark Heart.

"License and registration, please." I could just make out his malicious, self-satisfied grin.

I made a mental note that, if I ever got my driver's license (and right now, the prospect didn't seem very likely), I would never buy a Peugeot. Too many bad memories.

Like maybe *I died in one?*

I gripped Dana's hand, but my face wouldn't

cooperate with my grand plan to *show no fear.*
She knew, she had to know, that fire was like my
kryptonite.

There was an incredible sense of heat on my
skin, a heat I hadn't felt since I was three years
old and preparing to die for the first time.

"Is it hot in here, or is it just—me?" Dana
whispered.

"Oh, it's *me*," interrupted Beta. "And in a
moment you'll know firsthand just how hot I
can be."

"Can we talk for a minute first, Beta?" Maybe
I could buy just enough time to get Dana to disappear. And I had questions.

"About what? About how you seem to have
a habit of hiding behind your friends? Using
them as human shields? Ha! Daniel, you're truly
the most cowardly Alien Hunter I've ever met.
You'd embarrass your father…were he alive
today."

"You didn't know my father. Leave him out of
this."

"Didn't know him? Alas, not true. Your parents had me over to dinner on their last day, in

fact. They made some fine potpies, I must say. I fairly devoured them whole!"

If his manic ramblings hadn't shell-shocked me, Beta's evil peel of laughter would have. The flames roared louder than ever, and the car's side mirrors were actually melting. The glass would be next.

And then...well, it didn't take a Nobel Prize–winning physicist to figure out what would happen after the glass was gone.

Chapter 46

BY MY CALCULATIONS, Beta would burn through the car's exterior in a minute or less, and that would be it for me and Dana. Which would also mean no more Joe, Willy, or Emma. No more Mom, Dad, and Pork Chop. No more List of Alien Outlaws. And eventually, *no more Earth as we know it.*

I couldn't let that happen without a fight. But I didn't have anywhere to escape to. Beta was burning the car from all sides.

I tried every transformation I could think of; I tried teleporting, which I'd achieved on a few rare occasions. Even if I could make a hole in the roof, or the floor of the car, I would be traveling right through the fire. I could possibly coat myself in carbon dioxide, but how long would that last?

Minutes?

Seconds?

Could I do the same thing for Dana at the same time?

There was a whiplike snap as the safety glass next to me cracked all the way across. Then tongues of flame began to lick through the glass, reaching out for me like Beta's not-so-fickle fingers of death.

"Nowhere for you to go now, Daniel. I hope you prefer cremation over burial. I can't really offer you the latter option. Ha ha ha."

Okay, time travel. Now would be a great time for that to kick in, I thought. I'd rewind things a little, get out of this car, run away, get a job doing something a little safer — like deep-sea oil drilling. My father had said that emotion was the "on" switch...

So I did the most obvious thing that any normal teenage guy would do.

I kissed the girl I was crazy for. And I wouldn't stop — until I teleported, time-traveled, or died. Whatever happened, I knew this was the right thing to do.

Then the whole rear window fell away in a single piece. Beta reared back, ready to swoop in and incinerate me in a single blazing inferno.

I closed my eyes, gritted my teeth, said a prayer.

Chapter 47

IN MY MIND, I saw my father the day he died, felt the last hug my mother had ever given me, heard their voices chatting upstairs in the kitchen, unaware that The Prayer was fast approaching, that the happy life we had known was about to go up in flames, along with our strangely idyllic Kansas farmhouse.

In a way, I had been born out of that fire. It had forced me to become the Alien Hunter I was today. Maybe it was only appropriate that fire would kill me, too. Maybe this was my fate from the very beginning.

Speaking of which, *maybe I'm already dead.*

Chapter 48

I COULDN'T FEEL the heat anymore, or the car's springs poking through the backseat. I couldn't hear Dana panting with anxiety. And I couldn't hear Beta's crackling, hellish voice taunting me, either.

I opened my eyes... to see that I was lying on a gravel driveway in front of a very familiar white mailbox. Set back from it a little ways was a sunlit farmhouse. There was no mistaking it.

"Well, Toto," I said under my breath as I stood up, "I've got a sneaking feeling we're not in jolly old England anymore."

Unless this was heaven, or hell, or purgatory, or nirvana—I wasn't ruling anything out at this point—I was back in Kansas, at the very house where I'd spent the first three peaceful and wonderful years of my life.

This place was so full of history for me, and I felt like I was drowning in the thoughts, feelings, and memories that were flooding into my mind. I took a deep breath and asked myself *how* this could have happened.

My father had mentioned holes in time, created by powerful events. Well, I guess what had happened at the dump might qualify. But how had I ended up here? The only powerful event that happened at this house in Kansas was—

Before the thought had even finished, I took off running at full speed toward the house.

And that's when I heard the first shots.

No! Please! Not again! Please—not again!

Those were the same awful sounds that I'd heard time after time, in my dreams, on the road, making dinner, always playing in the back of my head. The deadly, deliberate "pop, pop,

pop" that meant my world would never be the same.

The kitchen was around the side of the house and had a back door that opened onto a small herb garden that my mother had been cultivating. I ran into the garden recklessly.

I remembered that long-ago day of murder and destruction like it was yesterday. The Prayer would be in the basement by now. Still, I hesitated before opening the door and looking in.

Then I had to *see*.

The kitchen was totally trashed, just as I remembered it. The wall opposite me was blown out and the table where I'd made my first drawing with crayons (a perfect copy of van Gogh's *Starry Night*) was in shreds.

But I had eyes for nothing but the two people who lay on the floor.

I remembered the last time I'd seen them, looking down as I left the house, a tiny, scared three-year-old disguised as a tick, hitching a ride on The Prayer's own fur. My mom and dad had been face down on the floor. Dead.

That image was *burned* into my memory.

But it wasn't how they looked now. My father was propped against the wall, my mother's head lowered.

I took a step farther inside, but stopped when my father looked up at me, right into my eyes.

"Daniel! Don't come any closer." His voice was barely a whisper. "You can't help us now."

I could only stare at him, but I felt my eyes filling with tears.

"I heard the portal open. It could only be you, son. You shouldn't be here, though."

"The Prayer. *I know he's here!* I've been waiting twelve years to find him." My hands balled into fists. "He'll pay for this, for everything he did to you and Mom."

My father shook his head slowly, with difficulty. "No, it isn't time for that. You're not ready. You have other work to do. Like dueling with Beta."

My mother stirred, her eyelids fluttered open halfway, and her face jerked in a way that twisted my heart. *She's trying to smile for me, isn't she?*

I could barely hear her, but I could still tell what she was saying. "Daniel...you've grown up well. I'm so proud of you. You're handsome, and you're brave."

"We love you, Daniel. We always will. Now, before he comes back...*look around you.*" My dad gave a gasp then and rolled over.

I stood there, sobbing quietly in the middle of our garden. The herbs I was crushing underfoot smelled magical. Thyme, mint, lavender. Everything I remembered of my mother's scent.

"Look around you." My father's last words.

So I did. I knew what I was seeing had to be real, but the colors and smells seemed brighter, sharper, like the whole rest of my life had been a dream and I was just now waking up into the real world.

There was crashing downstairs, and smoke began billowing out from the hallway that led into the basement. I backed up a couple of quick steps, the fire suddenly reminding me of Beta.

And how he had told me my parents had him over for dinner.

Had he—?

I couldn't finish the thought and only howled in more pain and frustration.

But then I stopped abruptly when I saw something more startling, strange, and beautiful than anything I'd ever encountered on any of the seventeen planets I'd visited.

Before me was a hole in time.

PART THREE
THE DARK AGES, MY VERSION

Chapter 49

MY VISION was blurred by tears, but the egg-shaped opening somehow shone clearly through them in an intense focus. It was about twice my height, reflecting a shimmering crystalline light. I could see stars, planets, and galaxies, swirling and coming together the way cogs and sprockets and springs fit together to make a watch tick—but here in front of me was the most amazing and complex timepiece ever.

I'll be honest. It also scared me. But you know what? Where I stood right now, with The Prayer's crashing and merciless howling, the smoke pouring out from inside, and, most of all, the two bodies that lay a few feet away from me — those scared me a whole lot more.

So I stepped into the hole.

And found myself falling.

It was the strangest sensation. I've been sky-diving a few times (none of them intentional), and this wasn't completely different. And yet... it was.

I wasn't floating in a vast sky or space, sightseeing the grand landscape below me. Instead, the painful Kansas scene was gone in an instant, *and now* the universe was rushing past me, giving me the gut-busting thrill of racing 250 miles per hour down a freeway.

Sound like fun? Maybe for a nanosecond. After that, my stomach felt like it was being turned inside out and licked by an alien with a spiked tongue. Good thing I didn't start to bring up my supper or I would've been wearing it.

And my brain — well, it felt like it was about to explode as it tried to take in thousands of images that flashed like 3-D IMAX movies on the walls of the wormhole I was racing through. Some things I recognized — wooden ships, warriors on horseback — and others were gone before I could even tell what they were — shadowy figures, patterns, supernovas of color and shape. Events seemed to flow in and out of one another deliberately. And soon, in among the images, I recognized something else.

Tongues of fire!

A series of multicolored, hypnotic flames writhed like a tortured prisoner. There was no doubt in my mind that it was Beta. And he was chasing me.

I saw flames dancing in gray clouds spit out by a towering smokestack. Fire licking at the remains of an entire city block, its wooden buildings nothing but cinders now. A field of haystacks, all of them burning to ash.

And then, eventually, one image: a lake covered by fire, glinting and sparkling in a moonlit night. Quite beautiful, actually.

A lake covered by fire?

Just as it seemed the fiery lake was about to engulf me, I suddenly gasped. It felt for all the world like I'd just been hit in the stomach with a sledgehammer.

I wheezed for breath and grasped wildly for whatever I could hold on to, hoping to finally halt this nightmarish flight through time. And my hands found something reassuringly solid, cold, flat — and *still*.

I grabbed at the earth.

Chapter 50

SHAKING MY HEAD rather forcefully, I found that my sadness, the deep, painful sensation that had been gripping my heart, had been blown away, left behind with the rest of the farm, and my mom and dad. Now I was lying on the ground, clinging to a few stalks of straw. The air was humid and smelled like summer.

I just lay there for a while enjoying the quiet peace until I felt a sharp poke in the ribs.

"Is he dead?" I heard a raspy English voice say next.

"Dunno," said another.

"Well, does he have any coin? May as well take what we can get from him."

Fearing the worst as always, I slowly opened my eyes. The two men leaning over me took a hasty step back, and I got a good look at them.

What the—?

These guys looked like they'd gotten their potato-sack clothes at a farmers' market—or a theater costume shop. They were covered in grime, and the ripe smell of unwashed flesh and body odor hit my nose. One even had horseflies buzzing around his mouth and hair-sprouting ears. I wondered if it would be impolite to point this out, and decided that since the same man held a nasty-looking knife, I would let his hygiene issues slide for now.

I squinted at him—and his weapon.

I don't know very much about the history of European armaments, probably only as much as your average European history professor. As a wild guess, though, I would have to say that this was definitely still England. And I was pretty sure—based on the shape and detail of his knife alone—that it was somewhere around AD 600.

The one with the accompanying swarm of flies smiled at me. I had time to count his teeth — all three of them — before his mouth snapped shut again and he pressed the point of the knife right into my throat.

"Oh, yer alive, are ya? Well, there's a toll for sleepin' in this field. Hand over yer money or this is going to be a real pain in your neck!"

I decided it was going to be a real pain in *his* neck, instead. No matter what year it is, teaching a bully a lesson never goes out of style.

Chapter 51

SEEING MY PARENTS die for the second time hadn't left me in a charitable mood. "Talk about wrong place, wrong time," I muttered, staring into Flyboy's bleary eyes.

"You can say that again, stranger," he growled. I savored his smug, sadistic expression as I curled my mouth into a frown and raised my voice half an octave. It's a little something magicians call misdirection.

"Please don't hurt me, kind sirs!" I pleaded.

I tried to look vulnerable and pathetic as I rummaged in my pocket. It took only a moment's concentration to whip up an authentic-looking medieval pouch, made of tanned leather, a little bigger than an orange.

He snatched at it like a frog after a mosquito, then weighed it appreciatively in his hand.

"Heavy!" he exclaimed with delight. "I think we may have hit the mother lode, Hubert."

"About time," Hubert spat — literally. And he was actually the more tidy and the cleaner of the filthy pair. "Now hurry up and kill him."

I heaved a dramatic sigh. "Well, kill me if you must. But count my gold before you do, just so I'll know I died a rich man."

Flyboy squinted at me suspiciously, but he untied the strings on the pouch, pulling the knife off my throat by an inch.

"Better be something good in here," he said.

"Trust me, there is. Something *great*, actually."

At that moment I unleashed all my concentration onto the space inside the pouch. The expression on Flyboy's face transformed from mean to surprised to terrified so fast that I nearly laughed. This was going to be quite a show.

I used his moment of distraction to grab his

knife. "I wouldn't want you to hurt yourself with this," I told him.

A wide gray elephant's *trunk* had popped out of the bag and was grabbing his throat, so he didn't care much about what I was doing. The trunk shook its captive, and the pouch flew out of the man's grasp.

Then the bag burst apart and a gorgeous gray elephant now stood before us.

Not many people know that elephants are aliens, brought long ago from my home planet as a gift to Earth. Of course, these medieval bozos probably didn't even know that elephants existed. And it was a shame, because this one was a real beauty.

Flyboy screamed as the elephant lifted him up like a marionette and tossed him a good twenty feet across the meadow.

Hubert, the more fastidious thug, had both arms shielding his face like he'd just witnessed the beginning of the apocalypse. "Swounds! What in the name of all that's holy is that ruddy thing?"

Flyboy groaned, and clambered to his feet,

growling. "'S a dragon, y' idiot! We robbed a bloody witch!"

Then he turned and ran off with his partner close behind. If they'd had tails, they would definitely have been between their skinny, grimy legs.

The elephant turned her enormous head, her ears flapping a little in the breeze, and winked a twinkling eye at me. Then she snaked her trunk into the air, trumpeted joyfully, and took off in a thundering run after the two would-be thieves and murderers.

Just in case you thought elephants were all sweetness, I can attest to the fact that this one had the time of her life scaring the bejeezus out of those dudes.

Chapter 52

MAYBE THE ELEPHANT TRICK had been overdoing it. I'd used so much power that I could barely even move my head now.

Not that I wanted to. A light breeze was playing in the grass beside my ears, and the air was sweet and clearer than anything I'd ever breathed in more modern times. I needed to start spending more time in the country—*the seventh-century* country, that is.

The only thing that made this scene less than perfect was a shadow across my face that was blocking the sun. A shadow that, now that I thought about it, hadn't been there a minute earlier.

And then a voice spoke. "Anyone who thinks an elephant is a dragon is lacking in wisdom, if you ask me. But those chaps were right about one thing. You are a wizard, aren't you?"

I did my best to crane my neck backward — and the boy standing behind me leaned forward so that we were staring at each other, only upside down.

I could tell that he was maybe a year or two younger than me, with sandy hair that was a little too long, and made him look like a reject from a 1990s grunge band.

Looking into his eyes, though, was like looking into a mirror. There was strength and intelligence, sure, but beyond that I could see anger, fear, doubt. This was a kid who knew what it was to lose something. I liked him already.

He laughed. "By the way, my dear friend, you're lying in a cow pie."

It was helpful of him to point that out, but I couldn't do much at the moment, so I just kept on lying there like an idiot.

"I know," was my best response. "I meant to do that."

He grinned. "Ah, I'm sure you did. And I'm the next king of England. Quite unlikely."

I squinted. "How do you know about elephants, anyway? You get a lot of them around here?"

"Well, I've never actually seen a great mastodon before. But my tutor's shown them to me. In books. He's a wizard like you."

"I'm *not* a wizard," I said. "I gave the thug my purse, and that elephant...just jumped out." I knew it sounded lame, but explaining that I was really an alien from the twenty-first century would probably sound a lot worse.

"Right, then," he said agreeably, reaching down a hand to help me up. "My mistake. What's your name?"

"Daniel." I brushed the remnants of the cow pie off my backside. Luckily, it wasn't a fresh one.

"Most chaps call me Pendy. I say, if you have time, might I introduce you to my tutor? I daresay he would be most interested in meeting another wiz — er, friend to the great mastodon."

I shrugged and smiled. If you know me at all, you know I usually try to avoid contact with strangers. Nine times out of ten, they're out to kill me. That other ten percent are probably trying to sell me beachfront property in Florida or Ginsu knives.

But there was something interesting about this boy. Meeting him made me think of my aunts, uncles, and cousins back on Alpar Nok—who, like Pendy, were all so genuinely warm and friendly and instantly accepting. My alien-radar was definitely not going off.

I wondered if I should tell him the truth—that I was a superpowered agent sent from outer space into the twenty-first century; that he would have to wait eight hundred years before the printing press was even invented, and another six hundred before he could read the very fine pachyderm-themed book called *Water for Elephants*.

But I had a legacy to fulfill and an alien—no, a whole list of aliens—to catch. I needed to find out where that fiery lake I'd seen earlier was, what it had to do with Beta, and finally, just what it was going to take to get me home again to save my friends.

Chapter 53

THERE'S A BIG FAT DIFFERENCE between having a mission and having a clue about how to execute it. Without my List computer, I felt caught short, and my powers were sapped.

I decided my best bet was to connect with Pendy's tutor. With any luck, I could draw out some info from a guy with some smarts. Scholars might be few and far between in the seventh century...who knew?

I was definitely unsteady after the thousand-year-plus travel through time. As I followed Pendy across the meadow, I was stumbling like a toddler who really needed to go to the bathroom.

Pendy helped me over a stile that crossed a stone wall, then through another field toward a river on the other side.

There was an island in the river, and a wooden building that stood on it with a giant wheel creaking and dipping in the water alongside a mill. We splashed through the shallows and went up to a little porch.

A white horse was tied to the railing outside, and Pendy grimaced.

"Oh, bother. Kay is here."

"Kay? Who's she?" I asked.

"*He's* my brother. Well, foster brother. Well, *idiot.*"

I grinned. Emma usually described Willy the same way.

The door was ajar, and as he pushed it open the rest of the way I heard a crashing and a cascade of centuries-old swear words ("zounds," "gadzooks," that sort of thing) coming from inside.

The mill was just one big room, with a rickety loft on one side, and a lot of cogs and gears on the other, which connected the waterwheel outside with a grindstone that was circling slowly around and around at about waist height. Beyond that, the whole room was filled with junk.

There were bowls and jars—many of them broken—and rusting metal cart wheels, animal figurines, half-eaten loaves of bread, animal bones, and on top of everything were heaps of paper covered with notes and pictures. There was even scribbled-on paper stuffed into the crevices of the mill machinery. So this was no ordinary workshop. Paper couldn't have been that easy to come by back in these times.

I picked up one of the pieces. It said, "Origin of Prometheus."

It struck an eerie chord with me. I knew the name, from the Greek myth about the origin of fire. *Fire*—it seemed to be following me everywhere.

Still screaming obscenities at one side of the room was an eighteen- or nineteen-year-old who must have been Kay. His sleeve was caught in one of the gears and he was on his tiptoes, being dragged in a slow, inevitable circle. He kept thrashing his legs, trying to get loose, knocking over pots and shields as he went around.

In his free hand, he held a crumpled piece of paper that he stuffed in his pocket as soon as he saw us.

"Well, don't just stand there, *nincompoops!* Get me down from here!" he yelled. "Immediately, if not sooner! Right now!"

Pendy ran over and lifted his foster brother up by the knees until he could work himself free.

"I'm going to burn this bloody place to the ground. It's a *death trap!*" yelled Kay the second he was disentangled.

I expected Pendy to offer some sort of comeback. But all at once he'd become shy and servile. "Oh, you mustn't be angry, sir. You know he doesn't like you being in here when he's not around," said Pendy. "Or when he *is* around," he added in a soft mutter that only I heard.

"Who is your dim-witted friend and why does he refuse to help me? Does he not value his life?" said Kay petulantly.

"Please, call me Daniel. And I do value my life, thanks for asking. I didn't know you needed help, that's all." I shrugged. "I just thought you were doing interpretive dance."

"I've no idea what you're talking about, but regardless, you speak with great disrespect. I'm a knight and a noble," he declared, fingering the sword that hung by his side in a ruby-studded scabbard. "I'm not a man you want to cross. If I cut you down right here and now, no one would bat an eyelash."

I grinned. He was less scary than he thought he was. "Looked like you were the one who needed cutting down, *sir.*"

Pendy was looking distraught. "Sir Kay, don't do this. Daniel didn't know who you were, and I'm sure he'd be happy to apologize..."

Pendy was wrong about that, but his pleas did no good anyway. With a growl, Kay drew his sword with ease. It looked like something he did a lot. And were those bloodstains on the blade? Suddenly I regretted my frivolous attempt at wit. I didn't have another elephant in me right now.

Kay pulled back, raising the sword high in the air.

Chapter 54

BUT INSTEAD OF COMING DOWN, the sword kept going *up*. Straight up. And Kay was still holding on to it by the hilt.

He reached up another hand, trying to pull the weapon back down, but it only shot up faster, finally embedding itself in the ceiling—with Kay kicking his legs at least twelve feet above the floor.

"*Kay!* You know I don't approve of violence. If you want to play, do it outside. *And far, far away from my workshop!*"

Standing next to us suddenly was a man in a red velvet bathrobe, grinning like it was his tenth or eleventh birthday party, and Kay was the piñata. And he was about as tall as a ten-year-old, too.

Only thing was, he also had a long, white beard, so bushy it would have put Santa Claus to shame. It reached all the way down past his waist. Which wasn't that far, actually.

Kay howled like an animal until Pendy ran underneath him, yelled "Let go," and broke his fall. Took an awful hit, too, poor Pendy.

Kay got up, dusted himself off, gave the three of us a long, dirty look, and stormed out, slamming the door so hard that it made a pile of junk in the corner collapse.

"That miserable oaf," the strange character said. "This isn't the first time I've caught him playing with my toys. It's fortunate I'm able to reverse gravity, isn't it?" The weirdo in the red robe giggled for about twenty seconds. It was awkward.

"He's just a jerk," I said. "So is anybody who needs to be called *sir*."

The bearded boy—or should I say man?—gave a start, as if I hadn't been standing there the whole time, then looked bemused.

"I'll be quite certain not to call you sir, strange fellow."

"Good." I extended my hand. "The name's Daniel."

"He's a wizard," said Pendy in a stage whisper, glancing at me apologetically. "Sorry."

At this, the short guy narrowed his eyes and stared at me. Actually, he stared past me and ran his tongue around his lips very slowly, like he was concentrating deeply. "You are *not* a wizard. No, no, no, no. That isn't it, not at all."

The next moment he winked at me, and I heard his voice very clearly in my mind: *You're an alien. What can I say? It takes one to know one.*

I reached out a hand to steady myself against a column, and it was a good thing, because he then announced, out loud, this little piece of news: "My name's Merlin. I see you and Arthur have already met."

Chapter 55

MERLIN AND ARTHUR.

King Arthur?

Merlin the Sorcerer?

Pendy was actually Arthur Pendragon, the future leader of England, the *legend*. A *myth*, supposedly. It was all too much to absorb at once. But then, I suppose the *legend* might be equally shocked to be meeting an *alien*. All depends on your perspective, I guess.

"Arthur, would you mind running along to the castle?" the little man—I mean, Merlin—said to Pendy—I mean, Arthur. "Daniel looks like he could use a cider."

Arthur, who had no idea that his tutor and I were both reeling from our sudden mutual mindfreak, trotted casually out of the barn.

"Well, that should keep him busy," Merlin said as soon as Arthur left the room, and then he burst into a series of delighted chuckles. "You look surprised," he said in his squeaky voice.

I didn't know what to say. Merlin blinked, and a black-and-white-splotched beanbag chair appeared behind me. I collapsed into it.

"Do you like it? I invented it myself. Just a standard cowhide full of kidney beans! Quite brilliant, wouldn't you say? Now, where was I... oh, yes! So I gather you now understand that I'm from another planet, and, judging by your... *interesting* clothes, you are too."

He looked like he was going into another laughing fit, so I interrupted before he could start.

"I'm an Alien Hunter from Alpar Nok, here to hunt down outlaws on Earth."

It might not surprise you to hear that this is *not* the most common way for me to introduce myself to strangers. It felt... good. But weird.

He froze suddenly, his teeth barely showing between his lips. "That's impossible!" he spat. And I do mean spat. "*I'm* assigned to Earth."

I couldn't believe what I'd just heard. Merlin was an Alien Hunter? Come to think of it, he did look a little bit like one of the cousins I'd met during my last family reunion, an annoying little guy called Syffaldingus.

"Unless…" Something seemed to strike him, and he stopped mumbling and buried both hands in his beard thoughtfully. "The future. Yes, that's right! That must be it." He whistled, impressed. Or at least, he tried to whistle. It just sounded like he was trying to blow out a cake full of birthday candles. "So I gather someone finally figured out how to jump between temporal rifts. Then again, I suppose I knew you were coming. Only I might have expected someone a little more, I don't know…experienced…to be the first."

"Experienced? You seem younger than I am!"

"I've been living here a hundred and seven years. I just imagined myself this way. A little trick I thought of one day while bathing. I call it *mentis vitae*—a mental fountain of youth. Clever, don't you think?"

I raised an eyebrow and pointed at his beard.

He shrugged. "Well, I kind of forgot what I was doing halfway through. I get bored easily. Mind wanders to other tasks, games of chance, foods I adore."

I shook my head. It was fortunate he'd never tried time travel. His short, skinny legs might have ended up two hundred years away from the rest of his body.

"You knew I was coming?" I said skeptically.

"Yes, yes, yes. Hold on, *where is it?* I know I left it around here somewhere." He got down on his hands and knees and started rummaging through one of the larger piles crammed into a corner.

All I can say is, Merlin would have been great at Jenga. He darted around like a mongoose, pulling out a sheaf of papers here and there, crude-shaped jars of ink and feather pens, a wooden recorderlike instrument, and the odd animal skin, tossing them a few feet and leaving all kinds of holes in the pile so that it seemed it would come crashing down at any moment.

"Brilliant! I was looking for this the other day," he declared. Without turning around, he handed me something. It was a kind of shallow clay cup, and it felt strangely warm in my hands.

"Hold this for me, my dear Daniel? We shall need it in another twenty or thirty years."

"What is it?"

"The Holy Grail, for heaven's sake! Isn't it *obvious?*"

Chapter 56

I PUT the sacred vessel down in a clear spot on a table across the room. Very carefully. But I couldn't take my eyes off of it.

"Say, Merlin," I began, thinking on my feet. "You don't suppose I could borrow that? I'm, um, pretty sure we could use that in the future, too."

"Hmmm...perhaps we can negotiate something, fellow Alien Hunter," said Merlin. "But first we must focus on more important matters at hand." He stood up to face me and smiled. "Here it is!"

His eyes were shining. I mean, they were

literally shining, a bright neon blue that gave his robe a purple luster. It was a moment before I realized that they were reflecting light from the even more mind-shattering item that was clutched in his hands.

I had never seen it before, but I recognized the form instantly. It was nothing like the laptop that I'd left in the London town house, but the thin leather-bound book Merlin now held out toward me had pictures that flickered in a familiar way, symbols that somehow ate their way into your brain. It looked a little like an ordinary high school yearbook, but the gold, flowing script stamped on the cover confirmed that there was nothing ordinary about it.

YE OLDE LIST.
Terra Firma.

This was The List of Alien Outlaws, about fourteen hundred years older, and analog instead of digital.

"*Ye Olde* List? Merlin, this has to be a *joke!*"

Merlin had only to open the book to prove me

wrong. On its yellowed pages, the words shimmered, and lifelike illustrations of devils, goblins, and gargoyles — which were actually *aliens,* I realized — danced in the wide margins. Literally, I mean — the pictures on the paper were *moving.*

Merlin pointed to a scene, and I took the book from him to examine it more closely. It was an inked black-and-white drawing of two figures standing on the moonlit shore of a wide lake. In the middle of the water, a huge maelstrom split the otherwise smooth surface like a hole torn in silk. At its center burned a small, ragged flame.

The whirlpool and the shadows that filled it were slowly spinning, projecting a rotating halo on the clouds overhead. And then suddenly the taller of the two figures turned around and looked toward us.

I dropped the book.

It was me.

And that wasn't even the most incredible part. At the same moment that I recognized my own face, a caption flickered into existence under the picture: *The arrival of Phosphorius Beta in the British Isles.*

"I hope you don't have plans tonight," said Merlin. "I do believe we have aliens to catch!"

"I say." I heard Arthur's voice at the doorway, where he stood carefully balancing three mugs of cider. "Do tell, chaps: what on earth is an *alien?*"

Chapter 57

MERLIN was good on his feet, I must say. He convinced Arthur that an "alien" was a rare species of insect that we had a mutual interest in — which we'd discovered after discussing the great mastodon. He explained that we were going on a hunt for the creature that night, but that Arthur surely wouldn't want to join us since "aliens" lived only in the smelliest and murkiest swamps.

Well, it wasn't *entirely* a lie, anyway...

Only a few hours later and closing in on evening, Merlin led me across the meadow on the opposite side of the brook, then into a dense wood.

It was just after twilight and the forest was the "dark and scary" kind, but Alparian senses are keen and the two of us had very little trouble finding our way through the trees. Merlin even skipped a little and, what can I say, it just reinforced the fact that I liked this ancient little guy a lot. Somehow, he didn't seem to feel the weight of the world, as I always did, on his shoulders.

"Now then, you must know a great deal about Beta," he said, spinning into a backward jog. "You came all the way here to help me, did you not?"

"We've met, yeah," I said darkly, my skin practically blistering at the memory of our last encounter. *Actually, I came back in time to help me,* I thought. And Dana, and all of my friends. If I could eliminate him now, I could return to the present, and Dana and I wouldn't be face to face with death.

"Right, then. I presume you know his history."

"I know that he'll be here in England for another fourteen hundred years. And that he won't be finished until everything on Earth is ash. You mean there's more?"

"Ah, that's not the half of it, Daniel the Traveler." He ducked just in time to avoid a branch and then straightened up again, still backpedaling so fast that I had trouble keeping up. "It sounds like they sent you unprepared...with no cheat sheet. This isn't good, not good at all.

"Let's see..." He sighed, the way a teacher sighs before launching into an hour-long lecture, then jumped like he'd been pricked with a pin, and spun around 180 degrees. "The lesson will have to wait. *We're here.*"

Chapter 58

"THIS IS WHERE HE COMES. There's no doubt about it, Daniel." Merlin cocked an eyebrow and his eyes sparkled with intelligence that went far beyond his childish appearance. "I calculated it very precisely. At least, I think I did. Couldn't find the notes I made, of course!"

We were on the banks of a small lake, its surface as smooth as a freshly Zambonied hockey rink in the moonlight. I was struck by a vivid memory of time travel. Could this be the same lake that I'd seen? The one covered with fire?

Merlin was pretty sure of himself and pulled me down into a crouch behind a thorny bush that stood near the water's edge. He didn't need to crouch, of course. Even standing on his toes, his tufted white hair wouldn't have shown over the leaves and branches.

We waited in silence. Merlin had hardly stopped talking, laughing, or moving since I'd met him, and so seeing this other side of him was downright eerie. I knew he meant business now. The Alien Hunter in him had come out.

After a time, it almost seemed like he'd stopped breathing completely, a sign that trouble was near. The slightest shift in air could mean trouble.

There was motion on the water. Even though the lake's surface was as flat as a mirror, we both *felt* it: the air molecules were vibrating in an unnatural, mechanical rhythm.

And then it slowly opened. A circle appeared in the center like a bull's-eye. Only it was nothing like the raging vortex I'd seen in Merlin's illustration.

It was more like a shimmering egg-shaped hole, with the *entire universe* inside.

A luminescent form reached out of it and

extended above the water. It was a wispy tendril of colored flame.

I gasped out loud.

A time traveler. Beta is a time traveler. The thought hit me head-on with the force of a semi.

Merlin pointed to the lake and we both watched as the flames continued to leak slowly into the misty air.

All at once, there was a whistle and a rush of wind, and then a burst of heat filled the cold night. The time hole was gone.

For a moment, a single fiery flower, twenty feet across, hung in the air. Then fire ran across the still water in a line that led away from us, into the dark woods on the opposite shore.

Before the flames disappeared from sight, I thought I saw a silhouette rise out of the bushes and follow the line of fire into the trees.

Merlin was shaking his head in disbelief. "A real live Phosphorian. Beautiful — in its disgusting, deceitful, destructive way. Never thought I'd live to see it."

I stood up without taking my eyes off the trail

of the invader. "So, what's the quickest way to follow him? We've got work to do!"

"Slow down, Alien Hunter," Merlin said. "I know where he's headed. And with time travel at our disposal, we've got all the time in the world."

Chapter 59

LIKE A LOT of magicians, Merlin could be really annoying when he wanted to. After his mysterious comment at the lake, he refused to say anything further. Not a peep out of him as we made our way.

When he guided us back to his *mill,* instead of the supposed lair of Beta, I threw a fit—but he just spent the rest of the night braiding and unbraiding his beard.

Well, *I* certainly didn't feel like I had all of the time in the world, and I was getting antsy. Part of me wanted to grab him by that stupid white beard, shake him around like a baby's rattle, and scream, "WHAT IS WRONG WITH YOU? BETA IS HERE, AND WE HAVE TO STOP HIM NOW BEFORE HE GETS MY FRIENDS! AND ALL OF ENGLAND!"

But this guy had this crazy idea that there was a time and a place for everything.

The next day Merlin mysteriously insisted on bringing Arthur and me to London. This was London *pre–sewer system,* and the whole place smelled like...well, yeah. Arthur had been nursing a black eye from Kay and wouldn't say more than a couple of syllables to me as we rode by oxcart. I'd been brooding about letting Beta slip through our fingers the night before and wouldn't say more than a couple of syllables to Merlin.

"Beta won't be going anywhere, Daniel," Merlin said under his breath. "And there's a *reason* we need to be in town. It's all part of making history. We can't mess with that, you know."

"That little crackpot!" Arthur muttered. "I don't have time for this!"

I looked at him appreciatively, and a grin

flickered on his face for the first time that day but quickly gave way to a frown.

"Kay left this morning," Arthur finally put in, "and if I don't repair his saddle by the time he gets back from his tournament, he says he'll give me another one of these." He pointed at his black eye.

"Why do you put up with him?" I said. "Foster brother or not, I would have punched his lights out—er, hit him. Smote him?"

"He never used to be this way, Daniel. But lately all he thinks about is taking over from Father. When Father's gone, Kay will be lord of the castle. And I won't be anything. Kay will probably turn me out onto the streets."

Somehow I doubted that.

"Out of the cart, young men," Merlin called to us. We were more than happy to jump out of the teeth-shattering set of wheels and were immediately distracted by the streaming crowd.

"So where to, Merlin?" I called over my shoulder.

But he was gone.

I hardly cared at the moment, I have to say.

That chipper, gnomish man-boy was getting on my nerves.

Arthur and I decided to see what the crowd was up to, and we were led to a ramshackle wooden church — really not much more than a tinderbox with a steeple. There was a growing huddle of people in the middle of the yard, around a very familiar-looking monument.

A huge boulder was half buried in the ground. Protruding from it, a sword hilt stood at attention. I almost fell over on my face.

A sword in a stone. *The* sword in *the* stone?

Chapter 60

I HEARD A MAN calling out as if it were a circus or the county fair. "COME ONE, COME ALL! TRY YOUR LUCK! PULL OUT THE SWORD AND BECOME KING OF ALL ENGLAND!"

Hmm. Not quite as romantic as they made it out to be in the books.

Right now a balding, powerful-looking blacksmith type was leaning over the sword. He spat in his palms and rubbed them together vigorously, ready to get a good grip.

As soon as he grabbed the hilt, though, the man's body went rigid and there was a *crack*. A moment later he flew backward a good fifty feet, like he'd been drop-kicked by Beta.

I took a step forward and got a closer look at the sword, only to be surprised by its, well, *plainness*. It didn't look like a great king's sword at all. The hilt was just ordinary metal—no encrusted jewels, no gold filigree...

And then I did a double take.

This was no sword. I recognized a certain, um, *Alparian* essence.

"Merlin?!" I said in my mind.

"Heh heh. Guilty as charged," said the sword back to me.

Chapter 61

IT FIGURED. It was exactly the kind of thing *I* would do. A creative solution to the problem. If I'd known there was a problem to be solved.

"I thought we couldn't mess with history?" I communicated to Merlin.

"I'm not messing with it, Daniel, I'm *facilitating* it," he shot back.

"Are we quite done here?" Arthur said at my elbow. "I'm not overly fond of crowds, mind you."

"Daniel, give us a little help here. Arthur's a very worthy lad," I heard Merlin say inside my head. "Just needs a little confidence boost. A little push. So, *push!*"

I moved a few steps closer to the boulder. Arthur followed me, looking bewildered. "What, are you going to give it a go?" he asked.

"No. Not exactly. *You are.*"

Arthur backed away as if I were crazy—or an alien, for God's sake.

"Are you mad? I'm a boy, a *stepson* who could never be king. I won't embarrass myself here. I will not do it."

I grabbed his arm and held tight. "You won't embarrass yourself. You will take a pull at the sword. This is the way life works. You have to try. You have to take a risk sometimes."

"No—*you* do it!" He held firm.

Oh man, I thought to myself. *What if I was the one who pulled the sword from the stone? What would that do to history?*

"I'm not...from around here. I'm not... *English,*" I stammered. "It wouldn't be right."

"Where are you from then, Daniel? France? Please don't tell me France."

"Alpar Nok," I blurted. "The United States of America. Either-or. Take your pick."

"I've never heard of either of them!" Arthur said and held his ground.

"Who's next?" bellowed some kind of monk standing near the stone. "Who will be king of England? Who has the courage to be king?"

I raised my hand high. *"He will be!"* I yelled above the crowd's murmur. "I'll go *after* you," I whispered in Arthur's ear. "And I have a tip for you too."

"What—what tip?" stammered Arthur.

"Wipe that other guy's spit off the hilt before you pull the sword out."

Finally, *finally*, Arthur smiled. Then he patted me on the shoulder and walked up to the stone.

"Well done," said Merlin inside my head. "That was exactly the push he needed. Firm, but not threatening. I'm impressed, Daniel."

Now all I could do was watch.

As soon as he put his hand on the hilt, he changed. It was as if Arthur was remembering something he'd forgotten since he was a child.

Courage *and* knowledge flowed into his face and flooded the depths of his eyes.

Whatever was happening to Arthur, the crowd sensed it too. In a matter of seconds they were whispering, jabbering, moving in closer to the stone. He didn't seem to notice. He was just staring up at the sky with wonder and sadness all mixed up in his face.

"He changed! Did you do that?" I whispered to Merlin over our telepathic intercom.

"I'm not that powerful," said Merlin. "By the way, make sure he doesn't swing me around too much, okay? I get motion sickness."

Then Arthur gave a mighty yank at the sword in the stone—a truly heroic pull—and out it came.

So what happened was history, not myth.

Take my word for it. I was there.

Chapter 62

I WAS HAPPY for my new friend and all. Really.

But I hadn't forgotten about my old friends, and my promise that I'd never put them in real danger again. And if Beta had anything to do with the fire at my house on that fateful day fourteen centuries later...well, I was going to get him before I got The Prayer—and I couldn't wait a minute longer.

So in the late evening of the first day of celebrations hailing the new king of England, I found good ol' Pendy and bowed deeply before him.

"My lord," I said in the most serious tone I could muster.

"You needn't call me that, Daniel. If you'd not dropped into my life—"

"Never mind about that. As long as I don't have to call you sir, I'm cool."

Arthur looked bewildered by the term but grinned anyway, and I told him I was turning in for the night. Merlin was still partying down— and let me tell you, the dude knew how to get jiggy wit' it, Dark Ages style. I figured I had at least an hour to sneak into the mill and dig around for some clues. Frankly, I'd had it with Merlin playing the Medieval Man of Mystery all the time when we had a job to do.

As I approached the mill I noticed a faint glimmer of candlelight through the window and stopped dead in my tracks. Was it possible that Merlin had beat me back? He was a wizard, after all. He could've zipped back on a broomstick if he'd wanted, although after all the ale he'd had to drink, I'd have seriously advised against it.

I was about to create some night-vision goggles but then stopped myself, remembering I'd need to preserve whatever power I could in case I ended up in battle tonight. If I'd learned anything from this latest adventure, it was to conserve energy. I'd have to use good old-fashioned stealth instead.

As I peered through the window I used no alien superpowers whatsoever — congratulate me — to cleverly deduce these three things:

1. The figure I saw was too tall to be Merlin. Easy one.
2. The figure appeared too pathetic and powerless to be alien. Didn't even need alien-radar for this one.
3. The figure had the same goal I did: to find some specific piece of information buried in Merlin's leaning towers of parchment.

As it turned out, the figure would make it a lot easier for me, since it took very little for this clumsy burglar to tip one of the towers. The material scattered everywhere.

"Blast!" he hissed, putting his candle down on the floor and scrambling to shuffle the papers back together. But then he stopped dead in his tracks, moving the candle over to get a better view of something he'd spotted.

"Ah, yes," he whispered, nodding as he committed the information to memory. Then, in a flash, he dashed out, the paper sailing behind him and drifting back down to the floor.

I didn't need night-vision goggles to see him in the moonlight. On a hunch I decided to follow Sir Kay to wherever he was so very keen to go.

Chapter 63

IT WAS ALMOST midnight. I had spent the last hour breathing stifling air in the pitch-black tunnels of a coal mine, which was actually a natural cave a few miles away, where the locals would dig up coal a basketful at a time.

I'd had to run into the mill and grab a weapon before setting out, so to my chagrin I'd lost sight of Kay's actual person very quickly. I'd had to resort to my extrasensory tracking skills, and they had led me to this place, though I wasn't one hundred percent certain he was actually here. It did, however, seem the ideal spot for Beta's lair.

"Figures it would be underground, dusty, and foul smelling," I muttered to myself. "More aliens need to stay at the Ritz." I suppressed a nervous laugh and squinted into the cavern.

As soon as I arrived, I'd felt vibrations far below the surface, and they'd been growing louder. Now their source was only a few hundred feet away, and closing in on me. With every tremor, streams of black powder cascaded from the ceiling.

An earthquake was the last thing we needed now. Mines like this one were full of explosive coal dust, of course, and if it was Beta…

Am I ready for him? I wondered. *How long would it take to run out of this place in the dark?*

The tunnel was really rocking and rolling now. Then, all at once, things got really quiet. It reminded me of that moment when the theater darkens and the audience stops talking right before a play begins.

But this wasn't a play. And the flames that were beginning to seep out of cracks in the ground weren't special effects.

I lay down on my stomach and watched the

space below me. It was easy to see the whole ballroom-sized chamber glowing on all sides with rainbows of flame. I could make out the mouth of a tunnel at the other end, fifty, sixty feet away.

Something was moving inside, a bright spark in the shadows. It didn't look like the wisp of flame that I was expecting from Beta — the one I'd seen *three* too many times already.

The flame was long and narrow. It whipped back and forth in the darkness of the tunnel like the arm of an octopus.

And there was a large body attached to it. I watched in fascination as a scaly, conical head snaked out from the opening, a lithe body like the fuselage of a Learjet following it on about eight tiny feet. We've all seen pictures of dragons, right? This one had lava seeping from between its scales and jets of flame for teeth.

The dragon scurried up the wall like a centipede, arched its neck, and took a bite out of a coal deposit in the ceiling. The sound of grinding rocks echoed through the chamber. Pebbles as big as my clenched fists rained down from its jaw. Then it cocked its head and gave a sniff that sent waves of heat my way.

"Welcome, stranger," it said in a familiar hissing rasp. "Please, come in. After all, there's no point in hiding now that I've *smelt* you. You can have the honor of being my next victim."

Chapter 64

I COULDN'T TAKE MY EYES off of the dragon — off Beta. It seemed like Beta couldn't take his focus off me, either. He stared down at me, and the flames where his eyes should have been glowed blindingly bright.

He was silent for a moment, and then he began to chuckle, his mouth spitting out hissing, gasping hiccups of flame. "You're definitely not who I expected, but I guess it's my lucky day. And that makes one of us."

I'd been waiting for this fight to start for days, but all of a sudden it was much too real for me. Beta's heat was too intense, the flames too bright.

And for some reason I could already smell burning flesh.

I froze. Just for a split second, but I definitely froze.

Here's a fact I've learned over the years: in the time it takes to read this sentence, an Alien Hunter who hesitated has probably been squashed and digested, or maybe vaporized two or three times.

I brought my weapon—one of Merlin's swords—up in front of his face. It was a basic parry, a way to block the opponent's sword from splitting your head open. Reflex, nothing more.

I knew that on its own it wouldn't really work against Beta's firestorm. It was time to start summoning my powers.

The tongues of flame hit the sword and ricocheted away, as surely as if I had been surrounded by a wall of asbestos. I'd created a shield of carbon dioxide—and lots of it—to stop Beta's flames inches before they could burn me to a crisp.

Beta roared in frustration and unleashed an even more furious torrent. This time I was totally enveloped in it.

When the air cleared, though, there I was, drenched in sweat and covered in a layer of black soot but none the worse for wear and tear.

"You're only making it harder on yourself," bellowed Beta. "I was going to flash-fry you, but now you're going to get slow-roasted."

"My dad always warned me that dragons were real," I shouted defiantly. "Descendants of dinosaurs. He didn't mention that they were buttheads, as well."

When Beta dropped low and sent out his next blast, I was ready and leapt backward, deflecting it deftly with my sword.

Now the fight to the death was really on. The dragon would spit an explosive fireball, and I would block it with a sweep of my sword. I would thrust mightily at the dragon's chest, the dragon would knock my sword away with a glowing claw. And once when I ducked to avoid a lash of Beta's fiery tail, it *cracked* like a whip and took out a stone column, sending rubble scattering across the ground.

Now, isn't this exactly what my dad trained me for on Cyndaris? Navigating tricky rock landscapes while multitasking—without falling? My dad had been proud of my training then, but he wouldn't have been now.

Because what did I do? Nothing but trip on a hunk of rubble with the edge of my foot—and I went over backward on my rear end.

Beta rushed forward to seal the deal. His mouth opened wide, his fiery jaws ready to bite off my head.

I saw it coming, of course, and the dragon's teeth met my sword's cold blade with a clang loud enough to shatter double-glazed windows. My muscles shook with the effort of keeping Beta away.

And then—inexplicably—my father's voice came screaming into my head so that it drowned out everything else. "Water, Daniel! Lots of water! Immediately—or you die!"

Chapter 65

BETA PRESSED his cruel face, his jaw, closer to my head.

My heart was pounding, ready to explode from my chest. I wasn't sure exactly what I was planning, but the cavern was *moving* again. With every motion of that huge serpentine body, I felt the hot stone tremble.

Dad had a good idea, but there was no way I could create enough water to put out Beta. Not in an hour. Not in a day. He should have known that. So just what did he mean? Was he back to giving cooking tips?

But then I felt something else. A constant

vibration, underneath the shudder of Beta's movement. *The rustle of flowing water,* I realized. *An underground river.* That was what Merlin was hinting about, wasn't it?

I put my hands flat on the rock beside me and sent my power surging through the walls and into the cavern floor below. In the next fraction of a second, there were three distinct hissing sounds.

The first was the mechanical hiss of the high-pressure fountain I'd just created, beginning to pump water to the surface at about fifteen hundred gallons a minute.

The second was the hiss of a gigantic water jet vaporizing into a cloud of steam as it hit a very surprised dragon in the throat.

The third was a hiss of pure malevolence. Beta's eyes narrowed till they looked like cinders, and he reared back onto his hind legs. His head was hidden in the cloud of steam that had already filled the top half of the cavern.

Gasping, I rolled to the side to avoid a swipe from Beta's tail, which was whipping around the room at random. Then I clambered to my feet.

There were a few glimmers up above, and an ominous clicking, as if Beta were trying to start a stubborn gas grill. Next came a blessed moment of silence.

But then an unearthly howl.

Flames swirled down toward us, splitting the cloud of steam in two. It took only a second before the fountain I'd made was a twisted lump of melted metal.

"DANIEL!" This time it was Merlin's voice. And he meant business. "WHAT ARE YOU DOING? It's supposed to be Arthur. It has to be Arthur. Do *not* mess with history, young man."

Chapter 66

"SOMEONE'S CHEATING," purred Beta from the heart of the fire. "I thought we were fighting *mano a mano.*"

In a flash my eyes darted through the cavern while keeping Beta in view. And there was Arthur, leaning heavily on one of the few remaining columns, with Merlin the Sword hanging by his side. His face flickered in the light from the cavern floor, which was lit up like the devil's disco.

I frowned. Merlin was proving himself to be the madman he'd always seemed. Arthur could barely stand up for himself when his foster brother beat up on him. How was this kid supposed to take out my *alien?* Number *3,* no less?

Then I remembered how I'd helped Arthur be courageous before. I could do it again. And had to.

I gave Arthur a penetrating look and encouraging nod that said "You can do this, buddy."

"Arthur, meet Beta," I said cheerfully. "Beta, meet Arthur. Sorry if there was any confusion, but you didn't give me a chance to explain. I was just the opening act. Arthur here is...*the real deal,* shall we say."

Beta had stopped roaring, but his jet of flame was hanging in front of Arthur. Then a dark face appeared in it, grinning in an all-too-familiar way.

Arthur didn't move, but I saw his eyes flick back toward me for a moment. Then he raised his sword.

"So, beast," he began, sounding more like a king already. "Let the tournament begin."

Chapter 67

BETA WASN'T INTERESTED in the grandeur of a tournament. Before Arthur had even finished his flourish, Beta's fiery jet darted forward till it encircled Arthur like a boa constrictor ready to squeeze and turn him into charcoal. Arthur dove and rolled and avoided becoming toast—literally. By inches.

"That was too close," Merlin thought at me, and then I heard him sigh, a long, long sigh of relief. So I guess he *was* a little nervous about Arthur after all. Was I just as insane as Merlin to let Arthur get mixed up in this?

Merlin wasn't going to take any chances.

At that moment I felt a sudden change in the air. The remaining clouds of steam began to glow white against the dark cavern walls. I heard crackling, and the sword's hilt began to glisten. I stared, trying to get a better view. Was that... *frost?*

Merlin was really something. Even I didn't know how to freeze water right out of the air.

And then in a beautiful stroke of luck or brilliant swordsmanship, Arthur thrust the frozen sword into Beta's side. The dragon's oblong face twisted in pain and anger and shock as its flames were sucked back in.

Then the huge beast slumped down, his entire body covered with a sparkling sheet of ice. His eyes, no longer flames, were more like empty sockets weeping frozen tears.

A tiny flame still flickered in his open mouth like a bright forked tongue, but the rest of his body was going dark.

Arthur drew the sword out of Beta's side and aimed for the dragon's head. This would end it, end Beta. And then the dragon's mouth opened and gasped something in a voice that sounded almost... *human.*

"I didn't think you had it in you . . . Pendy."

Arthur hesitated, a confused expression contorting his face. As he did, the last few flames leapt from the dragon's mouth, sizzled against the floor, slithered over to the wall, and—to my sudden horror—disappeared through a fissure.

"No!" I yelled. But it was too late. The last few sparks that were left of Beta had escaped underground. He wasn't gone for all eternity. He would rise again.

Meanwhile, the dragon's body was crumbling. By the time I reached it, it was no more than a pile of gray ash—with a shape inside, a shape that moaned and turned over as I came closer.

It was burned beyond recognition, but to my astonishment it began to regain its form. I saw Merlin off to the side, with both arms extended—chanting in an unidentifiable tongue. *Healing the beast?*

Instantly the form was complete—and it was human.

"Kay?" said Arthur.

"My king," muttered his stepbrother.

Chapter 68

TALK ABOUT A TOUGH DAY in the mines.

When we finally pulled ourselves together enough to hoof it back to the castle, Arthur locked himself in his room. Merlin and I had felt it was only fair to try to explain to him what had just happened, right down to our suspicions that Kay had become a flame weaver and that Beta had come to possess him. As you can imagine, that shocked him even more. I don't think he even bothered to sponge off the soot and burn marks before he turned in that night.

That gave me the private moment I needed with Merlin. I had a bone to pick with him.

My fellow *Alien Hunter*—or so he said.

I limped back across the fields to his house in the water mill in silence. By the time I got there I couldn't hold it back any longer. "*We let him get away,* Merlin. Beta slipped through our fingers! We failed. I've never failed like this before."

Merlin looked at me for a long moment before speaking. There were bags under his eyes that were way too large and saggy for his childish face.

"Beta is an extraordinary creature," he said, and heaved a sigh. "We had better sit down and have a drink. I suppose I'm going to have to explain this to you after all. Y'see, my boy, I'm not exactly an Alien Hunter. I was backup for one. She was my mentor. Guinevere was her name."

We sat down and he handed me a cup. It was empty. I looked at him questioningly.

"What? I'm exhausted!" he said, a little snappily. "If you want a drink, imagine it yourself."

I put the cup down as he pushed a book across the table at me. It was the same one he'd shown me before.

The List ... Ye Olde version.

This time, it was open to a page with a series of panels, kind of like a comic book. Only this one had panels that were beautifully outlined with gold leaf. The lettering was an intricate calligraphy. And of course the ink swirled as the pictures moved in an utterly dizzying way.

At the top, the title read "Phosphorius Beta— Known Aliases," and underneath each panel was a name in a different language.

In the first, a sinuous, cloudy form swooped down on a pathetic cluster of huts. It chased a group of terrified Asians around on the page, setting their village on fire over and over again. A single Chinese character underneath the picture represented the word for "dragon."

Another showed a bearded man with a sword and shield on the steps of a building with marble columns. Behind him was a grotesque creature that looked like it couldn't quite decide what it wanted to be. It had three heads, each of them a different beast, each more hideous than the last. The bearded man turned as if to run, but one of the heads was unleashing a torrent of fire that enveloped him over and over again. *Chimaera,* read the inscription in Ancient Greek.

In the third picture, a man in a feathered headdress was kneeling—and seemed to be praying—at the top of a stepped pyramid, maybe Aztec in origin. That is, until the giant, scaly bird-snake in front of him bent down and swallowed him whole, then let out a fiery belch.

The rest…well, you get the idea, don't you?

Fiery beasts of all kinds, terrorizing half the human civilizations I'd read about in history books, as well as a few that I didn't recognize.

Maybe because Beta had destroyed them?

I finished studying and sat back in my chair, confused, though a bit relieved. I'd half expected to see myself in one of the brutal illustrations.

Merlin slumped forward and buried his face in his beard. When he spoke, his voice was muffled, and rather sad.

"Well, now you can see it with your own eyes, Daniel. Beta's been ravaging this planet for all of recorded history. No one knows how long, really.

"When things get too dangerous for him, he

just hops through one of those time holes and ends up somewhere ten thousand miles and five hundred years away. That's what happened after he murdered poor Guinevere.

"In some of the places he goes, he's respected, even worshipped. More often, he's feared. But he's always looking for more fuel, and more power. The thing is—he loves to kill, lives for it."

That made his escape from the caves sting even more.

"But we could have stopped him in there. We could have shut him down for good," I said. "Destroyed him, maybe."

Merlin shrugged. "Don't beat yourself up too much. We did well today. He's never been thrashed this badly before. He's underground, licking his wounds, and let me tell you, no one will be seeing him for a long time."

"*A long, long time,*" I said slowly. "You mean like, say, fourteen hundred years or so? Sound about right to you?"

Merlin turned his head. "Hmm. Right."

"And he's still going to be waiting in ambush for me and my friend Dana on the other end.

With about a thousand flame weavers. So my whole mission here has been a waste."

Merlin thought for a minute or two, twiddling his fingers and humming a tune. Actually, I'd heard that song once, at my grandmother's house on Alpar Nok.

"Not so fast, Daniel. You haven't thought about what disasters you've prevented from happening here on the British Isles."

"Such as?"

"Imagine an explosion the size of the one you told me about that happened in your own time. In these times, Daniel, with so many people living in wooden huts with thatched roofs, with so much of everything we use made from wood and simple flammable materials...why, whole villages could be wiped out. In a thousand years or more, Beta could decimate our whole island."

"All right," I conceded. "So my time here wasn't a waste. And I made a friend in Arthur — and you, too," I added hastily. "But how am I going to defeat him when I get back to my own time?"

"Beta invaded this country once before,

Daniel. And the people who used to live here, the ancient Britons, built a machine to stop him. Guinevere and I helped them, actually."

"A machine? You can't be serious. If Beta came here before, it must have been hundreds of years ago."

"Try *thousands*," said Merlin. "I fibbed about my age."

"So what are you telling me? That this device to destroy him still exists? That it will exist in the twenty-first century?"

"You tell me. We called it *Stonehenge*."

Chapter 69

STONEHENGE. Of course I'd heard of it. A famous prehistoric site, the mysterious circle of giant stones on Salisbury Plain that has confounded scholars for centuries.

What was I to make of it? Putting my faith in a bunch of rocks to destroy the all-powerful Beta didn't sound like a good idea. But since when did any of my plans sound like good ideas?

Merlin and I talked into the night, but he couldn't tell me much more. Even if Stonehenge was some kind of alien Roach Motel, he didn't know exactly how it worked. "My mentor,

Guinevere, used to say, 'Look to the sky, look to the sky,' but that's all I can recall. I'm sorry, Daniel."

Too bad Stonehenge was pretty much the only chance I had, once I got home.

And that was assuming I could even get back to modern times. I could try getting to Stonehenge before the present day—but I didn't think I had the luxury of picking and choosing where the wormhole would take me.

The next morning, Merlin and Arthur brought me to the lake where Beta had first warped in. Arthur had been quiet all morning and I hoped he was okay. I'd told him I was going home, but not much else.

I regretted the talk Merlin and I had given him the night before. Gosh, would the king of England go mad on account of nightmares about extraterrestrial life? Merlin had warned me about messing with history.... But I looked again at Arthur and saw a sense of steady calm and knew that he would be fine. And a fine leader.

The sun sparkled off ripples on the lake's

surface. It wasn't as bright as it had been when Beta emerged, not by a long shot. But hey, I'll take serene landscapes over homicidal time travelers any day.

"Beta ripped open a gigantic hole here the other night," said Merlin telepathically. "I'll bet my beard that time is still weak in this area. You should be able to punch right through, Daniel."

"Yeah, it'll be a breeze," I thought to him, rolling my eyes.

Arthur shook my hand and fixed his eye on me seriously. "You sure you don't want to stay a little longer, Daniel? It might be fun. We could trade off being king every other week."

"You're kidding," I said, resisting a joke about trading off being Alien Hunter every other week. I sure could use a break right about now.

He shrugged, and the corner of his mouth twitched a little like he was trying not to laugh, or maybe like he was trying not to cry.

Part of me wanted to stay, maybe take him up on his offer. *A Kansas Alien in King Arthur's*

Court would make a great title for a memoir. But the rest of me knew it was time to go. I didn't want to leave my new friends Arthur and Merlin, but I had to.

I had a country to save—*this one.* England.

Chapter 70

NOW I JUST HAD TO MUSTER some really strong emotion, and open the door, on time again.

It wasn't hard to get emotional anyway. All I needed was one look at Arthur's face. The last few days had held more chaos for him than most people experience in a lifetime. He'd handled every one like a great king, and he was a good friend now, too.

Silently, the 3-D (or was that 4-D?) hole emerged from the water. Faces and galaxies and points of light flickered inside it, and Arthur's eyes widened at the sight. I could tell it was something he'd remember for the rest of his life. Merlin nodded and combed his fingers through the hair around his chin.

"I'm not good with good-byes, guys. All I can say is . . . stick together. You'll go down in history, and I'm proud to have known you," I said.

"Take care, Daniel," said Arthur, and then he winked. "Oh, and—don't let the *aliens* bite."

I grinned. "By the way," I added, half turning. "Get used to hanging around lakes. You never know when you might find a beautiful lady in one of them."

Arthur smiled back at me. "A lady in the lake. I'll be on the lookout. Sure thing."

Then I took a running jump off the shore, right into the hole, wondering if I was about to die a horrible death.

Hey, it happens more often than you'd think.

Chapter 71

I LOOKED BACK, twisted my head around like the girl in *The Exorcist* movie, but Arthur and Merlin were already gone. All I could see was a castle in the distance, with pennants the color of blood flying from its towers.

Like before, I was *falling, falling, falling.* I just hoped I was going in the right direction. I didn't particularly want to find myself in the middle of the Crusades, the Black Plague, the Spanish Inquisition, World War I or II, or a U.S. presidential debate, something awful like that.

Then again, the last thing I'd seen before going back in time was a car being enveloped in flames, *with me inside.* I wasn't too keen on going back there either.

I tried to look around and get my bearings—not that it had much meaning in this whirligig of motion and loud noise. Was that Dana's face, up above me near that odd tangle of DNA?

I craned my neck and reached out, willing my body to move toward her. It didn't seem like I had much of a choice where I went this time, though. Even in free fall, my feet felt heavy, and when I looked down at myself, I saw why.

Or actually, I didn't see why. *My feet weren't there.*

My legs just came together and disappeared in a single point above my ankles, the way they would have in some kind of crazy fun-house mirror. And more of me was disappearing by the second.

That strange, heavy feeling was spreading over my whole body, a tugging sensation that I could tell was impossible to fight against. I felt like water circling down the drain, fast, really fast.

I was pretty sure this time hole was about to spit me out someplace.

Oh, God, but where?

Chapter 72

UNFORTUNATELY, judging from the fact that my feet already felt as hot as metal left on a fire, I was about to arrive back in my own time, at precisely the same spot where I'd left. *I'll bet Beta will be awfully glad to see me,* I thought.

I strained and struggled against the forces that were ejecting me from the time stream, but it was no use. No matter how hard I tried, the car interior was gradually materializing before my eyes, or at least what was left of it. Every surface was blackened, and flames filled the entire physical space, like the air inside was on fire.

What was going on? Was I too late?

As things got clearer, the scorching heat became unbearable. I shut my eyes and threw all of my energy into twisting my body, not upward but sideways.

Then the ground knocked the wind out of me as I slammed into it at maybe 150 miles an hour. Just a guesstimate. But suddenly my mouth was full of dust. Maybe some of my bones were broken. Or maybe all of them?

One thing was clear immediately, though: I must have caused a spatial-temporal shift of some sort. I was not in the car. And I most definitely was not with Dana.

I hauled myself up shakily, using a stack of wooden flats as cover. I was still in the junkyard, and I could see the damaged hulk of Beta's spaceship outlined against the sky. A couple hundred yards away, flames cascaded skyward from the burned-out shell of the Peugeot.

Hallelujah! I wasn't returning home to the flaming jaws of death.

But—that meant—

No—no—no!

Dana was still *in* the flaming jaws of death? Without me?

Chapter 73

I SPRINTED to the Peugeot. I couldn't let myself believe it. Maybe this was a different car. There were junkers all over the place. It could have been any one of them...

But the hope was futile. I knew this was the car. And then I saw the telltale faint dark figure running off. The Dark Heart. He had just devoured his prey. I was going to take him out once and for all.

And so I went sprinting after it. My eyes were blurring with rage and tears. Closer, closer, closer... I was moving at a bionic speed.

But no one was more surprised than I when I actually tackled it to the ground.

It was a human being. Or rather, an alien being, one hundred percent Alparian.

"Dana?"

"Daniel?"

We gasped the words at the same time, breathless, and then I clutched Dana tightly and quickly rolled us off into the shadows, away from obvious view.

"How did you escape?" I croaked, still in disbelief.

Dana looked equally bewildered. "You sucked me into a time warp or something—right?"

"Unbelievable! We must've separated. I didn't know it was possible."

"What, you mean you didn't think it was possible for me to live without you?" she said with a wink. "Neither did I. And wait until you hear everything that's happened to me since I last saw you."

"I think I'm gonna outdo you on the

outrageousness scale," I said as I grabbed her hand and pulled her up and away.

The next part was easy. We decided to boogie out of there pronto. And as we ran, I could hear Beta shouting somewhere behind me.

"Gone? How could he be GONE? NO! I want him DEAD!"

On the last word, he flared up, blowing the Peugeot's roof high into the air.

I couldn't help but smile. Thousands of years old, but he still threw a temper tantrum like some preschooler. *"Typical guy,"* my mom would say.

As I ran even faster, I imagined a scene that would take place soon, when hundreds of Beta's servants would scour the junkyard looking for me. Eventually, they would find a message I'd scrawled in charcoal on the side of a rusty cargo container.

HEY, SPARKY,

I ENJOYED SEEING YOU GETTING SKEWERED AND FREEZE-DRIED BACK

IN THE DARK AGES. REMEMBER KING ARTHUR, MERLIN, AND ME? WHY DON'T WE DO IT AGAIN SOMETIME? HOW ABOUT AT STONEHENGE TO-MORROW NIGHT?

YOU BRING THE MARSHMALLOWS.

LOVE, DANIEL X

Chapter 74

DANA'S STORY turned out to be rather marvelous—but a story for another place, another time, another book.

But there's one important fact about it you need to know:

She met Willy on her journey, and he was sent back to the present time well before we got there.

Which means that Willy went through a time hole all on his own (another book, too). Now give me one good explanation for how that could happen? My friends, who I thought I created and controlled, were clearly having lives of their own now.

Things are not always what they seem, Daniel, and you still have quite a lot to learn, I heard my dad saying in my head. Wait a minute — Dad *was* speaking, but *not* in my head.

I was sitting in the backseat of a minivan with the fam, watching DVDs on a tiny screen hanging from the ceiling, and it was like my dad was reading my thoughts.

I had decided I couldn't face the ninety-mile trip to Salisbury Plain, the site of Stonehenge. Not just yet. Not after everything I'd been through. Instead, I'd created my parents, and then rented a minivan. I needed a little company, some TLC, a little downtime to prepare myself for Beta and, very possibly, death by fire.

And yes, I'd even brought Brenda along for the ride. She was chronically annoying, but depending on how things went tonight...I figured it might be nice to spend some quality time with my whole imaginary family. Now my dad was driving while I read a few books on Stonehenge in the back, and Pork Chop was watching, of all things, *Fantastic Four*. I knew why she'd picked that particular movie: every time the Human

Torch came on-screen, I would jump, and she'd laugh like the little maniac she can be.

"Brenda, don't tease your brother right now," said my mother after this had been going on for about fifteen minutes. "This is a very tense time for him, dear."

"I can watch something else," Brenda replied helpfully. "Let's see...how about *Dragonheart*? Or *Volcano*? Oh, I know: *The Towering Inferno*."

"You know, Mom is right. I could be about to die, Porker."

"Like I even care," she said, sticking her tongue out.

My dad turned around in his seat and laughed. "Hey! Do you want me to pull this car over?"

"Believe me, if I didn't have to go on this particular trip I wouldn't mind at all."

He nodded slowly, and faced forward again. "It's a shame we never got to take any trips like this when we were alive, huh?"

"Was there anything in those books that could help?" asked my mom, ever protective.

I shook my head. "Nothing I didn't already know. The stones are around four thousand years old, give or take a hundred years, and the whole thing is in ruins. No one knows anything about how the monument is supposed to work, or even what it's for. There are a thousand different academic experts with a thousand different theories about Stonehenge."

"Any of them mention aliens?" said Brenda, still staring at the video screen.

I poked her in the ribs. "Pretty much all of them."

"Don't worry," said my father. "If there's one thing you're good at, it's winging it. I don't need to remind you just how dangerous Phosphorius Beta is, though. And he is many, many times more powerful now than he was back in the Dark Ages."

My mother reached back, a little awkwardly because of the angle, and patted me on the shoulder. "But you're not so bad yourself, Daniel. So far, you're undefeated."

"Mmm-hmm." My father nodded. "Just remember, this is a single-elimination tournament."

"I get it, Dad. One strike and you're out."

Chapter 75

ONCE WE ARRIVED at Stonehenge, I sent my family away—just in case things got really horrifying. No need for them to see me die.

But then, guess who showed up? Joe, Willy, Emma, and Dana.

"I guess you guys are going rogue, now, eh?" I said, secretly thrilled that they were here, but worried all the same. "I can't tell you guys to just disappear?"

"Got that right," said Dana. "Don't waste your energy trying."

They were good company, since we had a lot

of time to kill. Hour after hour passed without any action from Beta.

"It's three in the morning. Maybe Beta chickened out," Emma eventually said from her lookout perch on top of a stone plinth.

"Yes, he's obviously terrified," said Joe, fingering the strings of his hooded sweatshirt. "After all, Daniel is a horrifying creature made out of fire, and Beta is small and...oh, wait, did I get that all wrong?"

"Thanks, Joe. You really know how to raise somebody's spirits," I said sarcastically.

"I try my best." But then he gave me a quick hug. "Hey, buddy, you know I believe in you."

But did I believe in myself? Against Beta? And his thousands upon thousands of minions?

There was a soft padding sound behind us. We slowly, slowly...turned...and saw Willy marching up from the ditch that surrounded the monuments. He was wearing a navy blue security guard's uniform. When he spotted us he shook his head.

"Still nothing. No Beta. No fiery demons."

I nodded at him. It *was* ridiculously quiet. No cars had passed in hours, and a fine mist had settled over the plain. It had made my clothes damp and my skin clammy. Dana, though, seemed as warm as ever, sitting next to me on one of the fallen sarsen stones.

"You feeling up to this?" she asked.

"Does it matter? I don't really have a choice, Dana."

"I just…don't want to see you get killed tonight. Or burned so badly that you're unrecognizable."

I didn't need to say anything to that, just nodded. A moment later, like she was afraid of the silence, Dana added, "He's made of fire, but he's not invincible. And Merlin must have sent you here for a reason. 'Look to the sky.' That has to mean something."

I knew Dana had to be right. But I'd gone over every stone in Stonehenge, and if there was some kind of hidden technology, I had yet to find it. So what had Merlin been talking about? There was no underground stream here. And these rocks couldn't shoot fireproof foam, or call down a blizzard.

"Well, whatever it is, it beats me. You guys have any ideas about the secret of Stonehenge? Maybe these stones are actually spaceships?"

"Why didn't you just ask some druids when you went back in time? I would have," said Joe. I could tell he was still sore that he'd missed out on my adventure with what he'd called "real-life dungeons and dragons."

"You know, Joe," said Emma, "this place wasn't actually built by the druids. It was around for at least a thousand years before the druids even came into existence."

"Really? I met one who says differently." Joe pulled his hood over his head and lowered his voice into a ghostly moan. "EMMA...EMM-MMAAAA. We druuuids created Stonehenge."

He started to climb up to where Emma was, still moaning, while she playfully kicked at him with one foot. Then suddenly she was all business.

"Okay...we got something. To the east. And it's *hot*."

Chapter 76

BEFORE ANY OF US could see what Emma meant, we heard the growl of dozens and dozens of engines. Odd shapes were approaching on the road, and they were moving fast.

Emma climbed down and Dana and I stood up, waiting nervously, straining to see what was coming toward us at a blistering pace.

It was a convoy of delivery trucks—like the one I'd seen at the metal foundry. There were close to fifty of them, along with six cement mixers. The whole train of vehicles must have been going at least ninety miles an hour. None of them had their headlights on.

My heart sank as I registered the massive numbers. I guess Beta had decided to show up after all. And he had brought some friends, or, I should say, some *fiends*.

Just before the convoy reached us, the lead truck turned its wheels sharply, effortlessly knocked down the fence at the side of the road, then skidded up onto the grass beside the monument. Barely slowing down, each truck followed until they were all stopped in rows, the cement mixers still in the middle.

For a moment or two, they just sat there, accompanied by the ominous ticking of cooling engines. Then the doors opened, and figures emerged from the cab of each truck. The drivers opened the rolling doors at the back of the vans, letting out more of Beta's faithful.

"Looks like Beta has a plan," contributed Joe.

Of course I knew what was coming next, even if I didn't want to admit it. There was a deafening whir, and fire began to pour out of the chute at the back of each truck, splashing onto the grass and splitting into flames the size of a person. Each raced along the ground in a random direction until the field had so many fires it looked like an army had pitched camp there.

The last of the flames from the three trucks came together into the tall orange blossom that I'd been expecting, and dreading. Then it leaned toward us, kind of like an old friend.

Before Beta could say anything, though, Joe piped up.

"What, you guys didn't want to park at the visitor center?"

Chapter 77

"HELLO, DANIEL." Beta sounded amused, even cheerful, but I could hear the menace underlying his words. "I must say, your note surprised me. I've spent fourteen hundred years thinking about how exactly to repay you for nearly destroying me, without ever thinking I would actually get the chance to. What luck!"

"*I'm* the lucky one," I said. "Now I get to finish the job that started in the Dark Ages."

He sniffed. At least I think that's what it was. "Maybe I should thank you, Danny Boy. When you forced me underground I had a lot of time to ponder the vicissitudes of life, and I realized something. Why burn a few paltry houses, or a few insignificant people, when I could have a huge, villainous army do the work for me?

"By the time I was strong enough to come back to the surface, I realized it was time to change my methods. Monsters were out, commerce was in. Cyndaris needs fuel, and Earth has lots of it. Have you noticed?"

"I've seen your so-called 'fuel,' Beta. You can't do that to the planet I love."

"*The planet you love?* Well, you're really going to like this bit of news, then. When my ships get to Cyndaris, you know what the cargo gets used for?"

I shook my head, knowing I didn't want to hear the answer. Actually, I didn't think there was anything Beta could say that would lower my opinion of him any further. But I've been wrong before.

He cackled. "*Fast food,* Daniel. Bottom-of-the-barrel grub. But what can I say? There are a lot of folks who don't care what they eat, as long as it's cheap and unhealthfully delicious. And fuel matching that description is just lying around for the taking on Earth! I would have to be an idiot not to take advantage! *Over one billion burned,* that's my motto. Should I give my ad agency a bonus? Or *fire* them?"

Funny how the aliens on The List never seemed to want to be artists or doctors. It was crappy movie producers, crooked used car dealers, sleazy defense attorneys, smarmy ad execs. And now this.

I gritted my teeth so tightly that it hurt. "Figures that after a thousand years the only thing you would have learned is how to be a lousy cook."

"Oh, I've learned a lot more than that. You and the boy king were lucky when you faced me more than a millennium ago. I was fresh out of a time portal, little more than a pile of embers. Now I'm a thousand and a half years older, wiser, and stronger."

I shrugged, purposefully nonchalant. I had the inklings of an idea forming in my head. "You don't look that impressive. I mean, come on. The dragon Arthur fought was bigger."

"Is that so? Well, watch this. Or just close your eyes, *and feel the heat.*"

Chapter 78

BETA HUFFED AND PUFFED, his flames pulsing in giant waves. Slowly, the shadowy face in the flames turned yellow, then brilliantly white.

The flame weavers standing closest to him took several steps back. A few shaded their eyes with their hands, which immediately began to blister and ooze.

As he got brighter, I noticed something particularly weird: the rest of the field was disappearing into darkness. The fires that dotted the plain were on the move, streaking toward Beta, joining with him. He towered higher and higher.

Then his core became so bright that it hurt to look at him.

Soon he was the only light source for miles. His flames crackled high above me, at least fifty feet in the air. Stonehenge is large in scale, with the tallest stones more than twenty feet high. Beta made it look like a toy model.

"You want big? I'll show you big." As he spoke, the roar and whistle of combustion tripled in volume until it was like a rocket being launched.

The human servants closest to him began to stagger. One man fell on his knees, then another. A woman fell to the ground, shuddering. Soon the whole field was full of prostrate figures, twitching and jerking.

And then, in a grisly reversal of what I'd witnessed at the Faust metal workshop, each body began to glow as Beta took back the fire from his followers.

"Is this big enough for you? Am I a worthy opponent now?"

Chapter 79

MY PLAN had worked too well. One enemy was supposed to be easier to deal with than a hundred, right? *Wrong.* I felt like a fool.

I clenched my fists and took a step back. "I'm ready," I yelled. *Yeah, ready to get melted faster than the witch from* The Wizard of Oz.

"You know," said Beta conversationally (if there's such a thing as a conversation with a fire bigger than a building), "I'm glad my flame weavers weren't able to wipe you out sooner. You know that saying? *Play with fire?* Now we're going to get to play in so many interesting ways."

Suddenly he leaned over—but not over me. Over Dana.

The force of his fire blew her hair back from her face. Especially with Beta's spotlight shining on her, she looked incredibly beautiful. Even though Dana couldn't help shrinking back from the intense heat, her expression was defiant.

"I wouldn't do that if I were you," she said.

"What was that?" Beta's flames lowered till they were just brushing the tops of the standing stones at the edge of the monument.

He didn't know that Dana was right, because Beta didn't know me. Messing with Earth is a good way to get on my bad side. But messing with Dana—that was the last straw.

I jumped in front of her, my arms folded. "Stand back," I whispered. "Get behind me. Please don't argue."

"What are you doing?" she asked.

"Fighting fire with fire," I said.

It was the only thing I could think of that might work, and something I'd never tried before. I concentrated hard, really hard. This was going to be interesting, to say the least.

Suddenly I started to grow and wondered if I could stop my latest brainstorm. In just a few seconds I was about 120 feet tall and I towered over Beta like a big brother.

I wiped the sweat off my forehead with my sleeve. "This seems a little less unfair, don't you think?"

Beta hissed and reared up, almost matching my height. "Daniel, let me tell you something. Against me, there is no such thing as a fair fight. Your idea is clever, but let's face it. It just means *there's more of you to burn.*"

Chapter 80

BETA DIDN'T WASTE any more time on idle chitchat. Suddenly he was a firestorm headed straight for me. I dove and rolled out of the way, but I'm sure I still suffered third-degree burns all over my colossal body.

"Hot enough for you, Danny?" Beta asked, and laughed like hundreds of hyenas on loudspeakers.

He was gathering strength again, and I waited for something else to happen, anything besides my eyebrows and possibly all of my hair slowly getting singed away.

"Funny you picked this particular place," he

mused out loud. "It reminds me of the first time I came to this country. Ah, the memories."

"Don't tell me you get sentimental about the places you destroy," I said, keeping my distance as best I could.

"Things were different back then," he continued. "I was burning mud huts instead of oil refineries. But England's always been one of my favorite places to terrorize." He sighed nostalgically, still edging closer to me.

"But all earthly things must come to an end, and eventually England will have served its purpose. Then it's off to somewhere else, and somewhere else after that, until this planet is a husk filled with ashes. I wouldn't worry, though. You'll be gone long before that happens."

I steeled myself, quickly coated both of my hands with carbon dioxide, and reached for Beta the way a cowboy reaches for the bull he's trying to wrangle.

Bad idea.

Worse than bad.

Worse than I could have imagined—by a factor of about a thousand. And that's saying something, because I figured grabbing him would be like sticking both of my hands into a blast furnace. Unfortunately, Beta was a blast furnace that knew what it was doing. Pain shot through my body like dozens of lightning bolts.

I let go and staggered backward. I had no other choice.

"I know, I know. I'm hot," Beta said. "If I could, I'd let you burn for a couple thousand years. It's the least you deserve. Flesh is so pitifully frail, though. Under the circumstances, I guess thirty minutes will have to do."

My arms, my chest, my legs, my back, ached. At this point, I wasn't sure if I could survive for five. It was so hot that the ruined stones around us were glowing a dull red.

In fact, the sky was glowing red, too.

No. That wasn't it *exactly*.

It was morning. The sky was glowing because the sun was rising.

And as the first rays hit the monument, something else happened.

Look to the sky, look to the sky. Wasn't that what Merlin had told me?

Chapter 81

FAR OVER MY HEAD, *another* sun had appeared, a hazy, red, shimmering orb hanging a thousand feet or so in the air. I'm not kidding you.

It was so faint I could barely see it. But I could sure feel it. Even with Beta's flames close enough to touch, this second sun felt hot enough to melt glass.

The combination was too much for me by a couple hundred degrees. I collapsed onto my knees, gasping, staring upward, praying for somebody to come by selling umbrellas.

"So. You've decided to accept your fate?" Beta

trailed off for a second, then began again, speaking more softly now, in a sort of rustling growl. "Finally you understand that you can never win. I'm too powerful to be extinguished now. Too hot to ... to ... "

Beta was silent for a moment, as if he was at a loss for words. His flames stopped closing in on me. I had a feeling he was looking up, too.

Look to the sky, Beta. Look to the sky.

"What...?" But the word came out slowly, in a low drawl this time. He sounded detached, almost hypnotized by the ball above us.

Was this Stonehenge's secret? The circle of stones, heated by Beta's fire, was reflecting the sun's rays, projecting them directly above us. Even in its ruined state, it somehow acted like a giant lens, focusing the sun's heat into a single intense point.

And that heat was attracting Beta like a magnet.

"The ssssun?" he hissed. "Thoussssands of yearsssss. How did I not ssssee it before?"

Beta's flames seemed to be reaching for the second sun. In just seconds Beta had become a column above me, hundreds of feet tall, drifting up as steadily as if he was on an elevator.

As Beta reached the transparent sphere overhead, he flowed into it, filling it with his flames. The hazy red ball became a burning white one. It really was like there were two suns in the sky, one just barely over the horizon, one blazing directly above me.

Beta flickered and spoke haltingly. "Wasss it you who made ssssomething ssso..."

As he struggled to finish the sentence, a sound came that was louder than any thunderclap I'd ever heard.

Then Beta's flames shot across the sky in a narrow line, straight toward the rising sun, the real sun. The fiery alien looked like a burning orange laser beam.

A single word came to me. "Beautiful?"

The sphere of heat overhead was suddenly empty again. The stones around me slowly cooled.

I guess that meant Stonehenge had done its work. It had sent Beta into the one fire even he couldn't handle: the sun. Beta was a pillar of flame, streaking across space, right into the heart of our solar system.

I raised my hand in a painful salute.

"Good riddance, Number 3. You're officially off The List."

And then I fainted.

Chapter 82

FOR THE FIRST TIME in what seemed like centuries—and it sort of had been—I felt something cool and refreshing on my forehead.

I opened my eyes.

Sweet Dana was bent over me, wiping my brow with a damp cloth. As she saw me come to, she sighed. "Thank God, you're tough. You had me worried sick, Daniel."

"Did Beta—" I began, and coughed. My throat felt like I'd eaten hot charcoal briquettes, several bags' worth.

"Don't worry. It was all just a bad dream," said Joe soothingly from behind me, and then he chuckled. "Nah, just kidding. You shot that freak right into the sun. Well done. You're getting better and better, buddy. Did you catch my joke there—*well done?*"

We all looked up. It was still early, and the sun was low in the sky. There was no trace of either Beta or the reddish hot spot that had led to his sudden departure from Earth.

"You think he'll survive up there?" said Dana after a while.

I shook my head. "Beta's hot, but the sun is hotter. I think it would be like trying to get a glass of water back after pouring it into the ocean."

I sat up finally. My head felt like it might have a big lump on the back, but I couldn't rub it. My hands and wrists were swollen and raw and already blistering.

"We're lucky Stonehenge was still in good working order," Dana said, and looked around.

"Yeah." I sighed. "Even with half the stones missing, it was enough. Payback. Four thousand years in the making. Worth the wait."

"Three cheers for the ancient Brits," said

Emma, eyeing Joe like she was daring him to mention the druids.

"By the way," said Willy, nodding at the fields beyond the monument, "what are we gonna do about *them?*"

Around the trucks still parked on the grass, Beta's minions, hundreds of them, were tossing and turning, and looked to be in some real pain. Quite a few were just sitting, holding their knees, rocking back and forth.

"I think they'll be all right eventually. They'll just have to get used to living their own lives again," I said.

Dana smiled at me. "Well, I hope you're proud of yourself, Daniel. You saved the world, again. Or at least England. Now, didn't I remember someone saying something about a vacation?"

She pulled me to my feet, and the five of us walked slowly back to the rental van, still parked in the visitor center lot where my father had left it. As we piled in, I looked back. Salisbury Plain was streaked with tire tracks. The ancient stones were scorched and blackened, and in the middle of them was a huge crater.

When the English Heritage people got here in a few hours, they wouldn't be too happy. Which was a shame, in a way, since Stonehenge had finally completed its task.

It had saved England.

EPILOGUE
ANYONE FOR CHOCOLATE CROISSANTS?

Chapter 83

WHOEVER SAYS that the English Channel is too bloody freezing cold should go up against a Cyndarian like Beta sometime. After the battle at Stonehenge, I couldn't get enough of the cold. Ice cream, air-conditioning—and now an invigorating swim.

It's twenty-one miles from England to France, and the best swimmers in the world can do it in about seven hours. At the rate we were going, we would do it in less than two.

We were cheating, a little: I'd made wet suits to keep us a bit warmer and help us float. But, hey, it's not like we were trying to break any official world records. This was strictly off-the-books stuff. Like everything I do.

I was feeling quite a bit better. My mother had taken good care of me, and my burns were mostly healed. Yep, *that* fast.

Still, I didn't think I'd be doing much baking for a while.

"I don't really get it," said Joe between breaths. "Even if Stonehenge was built to be some kind of thermal lens, like you say, how did it shoot Beta into space?"

"I'm not sure it did," I said, turning on my side. "He almost sounded like he wanted to go. Like once he felt the sun's heat, he couldn't help it. A moth to a flame, or something like that. What do I know about thermonuclear physics?"

Joe shrugged, which made him sink, and whatever he said next came out as bubbles.

"All right, I've got a better question," said Dana, changing the subject. "What part of our vacation are you guys looking forward to the most?"

"No question. Lunch on the Champs-Elysées!" said Willy. "The French do their meals right. A little pâté, a baguette, some fantastic cheese, and those folks never seem to get fat."

"The best pastries in the world," said Emma. "I could go for a chocolate croissant."

"I can't wait to get there," said Willy. "I know...last one to France foots the bill!" On that note he launched himself into an energetic freestyle. As if they could already smell the food, Emma and Joe took off after him.

Dana, floating lazily on her back, smiled at me. "You know, Daniel, that fight the other night gave you an incredible tan. In Hollywood they'd shell out big bucks to anyone who looks as good as you do."

I cocked my head at her. "You think?"

Dana's eyes twinkled. She flipped over again and dove underwater with the grace of a dolphin, kicking hard to catch up with the others before she came to the surface again.

"No, not really, Daniel," she called back to me. "If anything, you look like you should be headed to the nearest burn ward." She laughed—a sound that was better than music, even Mozart.

It was like a kind of magic.

A kind of magic that even Merlin couldn't touch in a million time-warped years.

And neither would any other alien, ever.

I swear.

You'll need the Ultimate Power to take on the scum of the Earth!

From Best-Selling Author
JAMES PATTERSON

Additional
Nintendo DSi™
Feature

DANIEL X
THE ULTIMATE POWER

Daniel X was born with the greatest superpower of all, the power to create. Now, the fate of the world rests on his shoulders—saving the world has never been easy, but it's a fight Daniel is made for.

CREATE: Conquer aliens from "The List" by changing into an eagle and soar your way to victory.

EXPLORE: Solve intriguing puzzles and discover new areas within the alien universe while battling your way back to Earth.

FIGHT: Battle a myriad of relentless enemies using wits, strength and speed.

An all new DanielX Adventure for Nintendo DSi™/DS™

www.thq.com

GRIPTONITE.

Get it Today!